"W _and get the hell out of my room?"_

Marlie finally managed to get out.

Well, hell. They were back to this. "Marlie," Caid said patiently, "I told you last night who I am. Remember?"

"Caid?" Her tone sounded disbelieving.

"Yeah. Caid Matthews."

"Caid Matthews, you're naked as a jaybird! Get out of my room!" Marlie screeched, throwing a pillow at him.

But Caid didn't move. "You can _see_ me?"

Marlie finally seemed to grasp the importance of the moment. She blinked, then slowly, wickedly grinned. "Yes, Caid, I can _definitely_ see you."

Dear Reader,

October is bringing big changes in the Silhouette and Harlequin worlds. To strengthen the terrific lineup of stories we offer, Silhouette Romance will be moving to four fabulous titles each month.

Don't miss the newest story in this six-book series— MARRYING THE BOSS'S DAUGHTER. In this second title, *Her Pregnant Agenda* (#1690) by Linda Goodnight, Emily Winters is up to her old matchmaking tricks. This time she has a bachelor lawyer and his alluring secretary—a single mom-to-be—on her matrimonial short list.

Valerie Parv launches her newest three-book miniseries, THE CARRAMER TRUST, with *The Viscount & the Virgin* (#1691). In it, an arrogant royal learns a thing or two about love from his secret son's sassy aunt. This is the third continuation of Parv's beloved Carramer saga.

An ornery M.D. is in danger of losing his heart to a sweet young nurse, in *The Most Eligible Doctor* (#1692) by reader favorite Karen Rose Smith. And is it possible to love a two-in-one cowboy? Meet the feisty teacher who does, in Doris Rangel's magical *Marlie's Mystery Man* (#1693), our latest SOULMATES title.

I encourage you to sample all four of these heartwarming romantic titles from Silhouette Romance this month.

Enjoy!

Mavis C. Allen
Associate Senior Editor, Silhouette Romance

Please address questions and book requests to:
Silhouette Reader Service
U.S.: 3010 Walden Ave., P.O. Box 1325, Buffalo, NY 14269
Canadian: P.O. Box 609, Fort Erie, Ont. L2A 5X3

Marlie's
Mystery Man

DORIS RANGEL

SILHOUETTE _Romance_®

Published by Silhouette Books

America's Publisher of Contemporary Romance

For the TMTW faithful and the mountains
that keep me coming home.

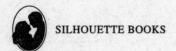 SILHOUETTE BOOKS

ISBN 0-373-19693-8

MARLIE'S MYSTERY MAN

This edition published by arrangement with Harlequin Books S.A.

® and TM are trademarks of Harlequin Books S.A., used under license.
Trademarks indicated with ® are registered in the United States Patent
and Trademark Office, the Canadian Trade Marks Office and in other
countries.

Visit Silhouette at www.eHarlequin.com

Printed in U.S.A.

Books by Doris Rangel

Silhouette Romance

Marlie's Mystery Man #1693

Silhouette Special Edition

Mountain Man #1140
Prenuptial Agreement #1224

DORIS RANGEL

loves books…the feel of them, the sight of them, the smell of them. And she loves talking about them. She has collected them, organized them, sold them new and used, written them, worked with others to write them, read them aloud to children and has hopefully imparted the magic of them to the grade school, college and adult students she has taught over the years. History, philosophy, science, satire, Western, mystery… In her home, books are the wallpaper of choice.

Romances hold a special place on her shelves, however. A story that ends with a couple stepping into the future with love and hope may be an ideal, but it is an ideal she wishes for the tomorrows of every living thing in the universe. Love, after all, in whatever form it takes, is all that is.

Doris enjoys hearing from readers and you may contact her via snail mail at P.O. Box 5645, Victoria, TX 77903-5645, or via e-mail at Drangel@selectrec.net.

All underlined places are fictitious.

Prologue

"*Hell, I can't fire Waldo! He's been ramrod on the Rolling M since before I was born.*"

Snorting angrily, Caid Matthews down-shifted the pickup to climb another steep grade.

"*He's eighty, dammit, and I'm not firing him. Dad gave him a good retirement package. And it's not like he'll have to live on the streets. He can move to Florida, like he always said he would. Flirt with the blue-haired widows. Maybe marry one.*"

"*Sure that's what he says, but everybody knows that's just talk. Waldo's lived in West Texas all his life, most of it in the Davis Mountains as a hand on the Rolling M. The day he shucks his Levi's for swimming trunks is the day the sun stands still.*"

Caid sighed and used a knuckle to rub the bridge of his nose. He'd been fighting with himself over this for the past week, his brain knowing the ranch could no longer afford Waldo's salary, but his heart knowing it would kill the old man to leave the Rolling M.

And it wasn't just Waldo. The Rolling M's finances were in deep horse hockey in a way they'd never been before. Caid had trimmed everywhere he could find to trim, with part of him knowing it had to be done and the other part madder than hell that he had to do it.

Waldo had to go. There was no other way. And five hundred acres had to go, too. That five hundred acres might be only a drop in the Rolling M's proverbial bucket, but never in the history of the ranch had any acreage been sold.

Though he knew there was no alternative, Caid often felt like his soul was being ripped in two.

The pickup topped the grade and settled into the long glide toward a wide valley below where he'd have several miles of flat. Good. Now he could make up time.

Hell of a thing. He'd driven from the ranch all the way to Fort Davis, even checked into the hotel so he could be at the bank first thing in the morning.

But he'd no sooner placed his duffel bag beside the bed than he realized he'd left the papers he needed for the bank on the kitchen table.

There was nothing else to do but return to the ranch and get them, then make the long drive back to town.

Just went to show the state of mind he was in lately. He'd never been this forgetful. Why, he'd even left his hat with his lucky jay feather back in the hotel room.

Now on the flats, Caid sent the ancient truck flying down the highway. The sun was low in the west and he hadn't passed another vehicle in the last twenty miles—not unusual in this part of Texas.

"You ever stop to think that leaving those papers might be a way of telling you something?"

Caid shook his head angrily, wishing he could somehow yank his other, softer side completely out of his body. This constant inner debate with himself interfered with every decision he knew he had to make.

"I've got to sell and that's all there is to it. It's that or lose the whole damn ranch. I'm doing what I have t—"

A deer! Stepping right into the headlights.

With no shoulder to the road, he swerved off the highway completely to avoid the petrified animal. By the grace of God and three good inches, he missed it.

Unfortunately, he didn't miss the sixty-year-old ponderosa pine.

"Your man is a western man, honey."

"Oh, Gram. Please. I'm going to West Texas for a vacation, not another man. After Nicholas, I can't think of anything I want less."

"The Great Ones don't care if you want him or not, Marlie. They just told me he's in Fort Davis. Take him or leave him, it's yours to decide."

"I'll leave him, then, but you can tell The Great Ones thanks for the playmate while I'm there. Just warn them that I'm not bringing home any souvenirs."

"Don't be flip, dear. It's not becoming. Besides, the heart has a mind of its own."

"Sounds like a country-western song, Gram. And I don't have a heart anymore. Nicholas threw it out with yesterday's leftovers."

Recalling the conversation she'd had with her grandmother before leaving San Antonio, Marlie smiled grimly to herself and signaled to exit the interstate. Forty more miles and she'd be in the picturesque little town of Fort Davis where she planned to get a grip.

Forty extremely dark miles. The state highway had even less traffic than I-10, and led her through the kind of darkness San Antonio hadn't experienced for over a century. A million stars spangled the sky.

Gradually, however, the stars along the horizon blotted into a jagged line that Marlie assumed were the Davis Mountains. The road twisted and turned as it wound among them, slowing her driving to a nervous crawl.

Marlie's neck and shoulders ached with tension and exhaustion.

Sighing, she thought of the brightly lit motel she'd passed eighty miles behind her.

She'd almost stopped. Why hadn't she? After all, she didn't have hotel reservations to keep. Her friend, Jill, who had recommended Fort Davis as a great place to relax and hike—a good place to recover, she'd meant—had said reservations weren't necessary this time of year.

Yet Marlie had passed up the motel and was now figuratively kicking herself for it.

This was supposed to be a vacation, not an endurance race. It didn't *matter* if she spent the night in Fort Davis, for Heaven's sake! Yet here she was, seven hours out of San Antonio and eighty miles past common sense.

Her part Native American grammie would say The

Great Ones guided her. But then, Gram didn't like to admit that any of her family were stupid. Stupid over men, stupid over sticking her nose into what was none of her business.

To Gram, descended from a noted shaman, everything was a sign. Take the blue feather that now rested in Marlie's shirt pocket, for instance.

After uncharacteristically stalling her with errands and lunch and cleaning the kitchen, Gram had finally allowed Marlie to head out the door to get her vacation underway.

She'd placed a loving arm around Marlie's shoulders and walked her to the car. "You'll see," the older woman said. "Your happiness is in the west, sweetness. Look. Here's your sign."

Following Gram's pointing finger, Marlie obligingly looked down. A small blue feather lay on the concrete drive right beside the car door.

"Take it with you, dear. Your man has the other one."

But Marlie had hesitated before picking it up.

The family had a saying: "When you're going on a trip, never accept one of Gram's little presents if she didn't buy it." All of them knew strange things happened when Gram decided to give "just a little something" from her own possessions.

Not bad things, mind you, but…strange ones.

So far, Grammie's "little somethings" had brought into the family two husbands, a wife, a baby, a pet iguana and a 1970s VW bus for a delighted teenager—all of which came at considerable surprise to the cousins involved who had thought they were merely going from Point A to Point B for a little R and R.

Still, Marlie reasoned, the feather was a found object, not truly a gift. It ought to be safe.

She picked it up. The vibrant blue of the feather seemed to glow against her palm.

How very appropriate, she had thought. *My bluebird of happiness is molting.*

Fort Davis, two miles. Thank God.

Chapter One

Marlie's eyes popped open.

Something had wakened her. What?

And then she knew.

Coming from nowhere, from everywhere, a soft, elongated groan seemed to fill the hotel room. With her heart slowing to a shallow, desperate chugging, Marlie held her breath, which wasn't easy when what she really wanted to do was scream.

Inch by cautious inch, she sat up to peer into the darkness, but only the clock on the bedside table had any substance. Twelve thirty-six, it declared precisely in bilious, luminescent green.

Another soft groan floated into the darkness and Marlie gasped, yet squint as she might, she couldn't see a thing.

Clutching the blankets to her chin, she considered hurling them over her head. Hey, it worked, didn't it? Certainly the maneuver had taken care of monsters when she was a kid.

The eerie sound began again, starting on a soft note then gathering strength for another stretch of oral misery. Yep, she was heading under the covers.

Suddenly, however, the building ooo-ooohs snorted and strangled and gasped themselves into an explosive and decidedly damp *Ker-choo!*

Ghosts don't sneeze!

Without thinking, Marlie reached out a hand and switched on the bedside lamp.

The room was empty.

Her gaze swung to the door, but the chain was still on, the deadbolt still in place. The room's one window was up, but only about three inches, the exact amount Marlie had raised it. Surely no self-respecting intruder would come through a window, then close it behind him once he was in the room. Besides, she was on the second floor.

The second double bed, a match to the old-fashioned iron one she slept in, was a mess of sheets and blankets, the way it had been when she arrived only a half hour before. Marlie hadn't minded.

Her friend Jill's blithe assertion that she wouldn't need reservations had been sadly mistaken. A large amateur astronomy group was in the area and the star-gazers who weren't camping filled every available room in town.

Marlie had tried every hotel in Fort Davis, but only Ann, the desk clerk at the Hotel Limpia, had taken pity on her after one look at Marlie's exhausted face.

By chance, the Limpia did have a room, Ann told her. It seemed its former occupant had checked in but left the room almost immediately. Unfortunately, he'd been involved in an automobile accident and was now in the hospital.

Since the room had been secured with a credit card but not actually paid for, Marlie could have it if she didn't mind it being briefly used by someone else and therefore not in the hotel's usual pristine condition.

Marlie didn't mind, but would the former occupant?

Ann had laughed, saying the man was a local and an old school friend who would like even less being charged for a room he didn't use.

Breathing a sigh of relief, Marlie took it.

When she was shown to the room at the end of the old-fashioned hall upstairs—a double; the man, too, had taken what he could get—a duffel bag still sat on the floor beside one of the two beds. The bed itself was heavily disarranged, but when Ann went to straighten it, Marlie told her not to bother. She would be sleeping in the other one anyway.

The desk clerk left, taking the man's bag and toiletries with her and giving a last apology for the used towels in the bathroom. There were clean ones in the cabinet.

By then so tired she felt like a wet noodle, Marlie simply pulled off her clothes, slathered herself with lotion and tumbled into the untouched bed. She was not so exhausted, however, that she hadn't known for a positive fact there was no one in the room but herself.

Yet the moan had sounded so close.

Slowly, cautiously, Marlie leaned over the edge of her bed to peer under it.

Nada. Not even a dust bunny.

But while she was bent over, practically standing on

her head with her rump still on the mattress, another massive sneeze made her jump so hard she had to catch herself to keep from tumbling onto the floor. She whipped upright, only to hear a sniff of what clearly had to be congestion…then, incredibly, the sound of someone honking into a handkerchief or tissue.

Another moan, a short one this time. A sigh. Another sniff.

Silence.

And there was no one but herself in the room!

Absolutely stunned, Marlie leaned slowly back against the pillows—and reality struck.

This was an old hotel, built around the turn of the century, Ann had said. Old hotels had thin walls. A man—it was definitely a masculine sneeze—in the next room had a cold and didn't mind moaning and groaning about it.

Mystery solved.

Letting out a relieved sigh and feeling a little foolish, Marlie clicked off the lamp and snuggled back under the warmth of the covers.

But just as her eyes drifted blissfully shut, she heard a sniff and another low moan, though now the sounds seemed muffled, as if whoever it was had turned his face into a pillow.

Thanks be for that, Marlie thought sleepily, and did no more thinking at all until she awoke early the next morning to the sound of birdsong and what Fort Davis called traffic.

Caid swung his legs over the side of the bed and immediately clutched his head with both hands to keep it anchored to his shoulders.

God, it hurt. He probably had a mild concussion.

Too bad. He didn't have time to see a doctor. What would a doctor tell him anyway but to stay quiet, drink plenty of liquids, etcetera, and don't take any naps? But, though he didn't remember actually getting into bed, he *had* slept and hadn't wakened up dead, so no problem there except the headache from hell.

And his allergies giving him fits.

The thought of breakfast made him queasy, but he'd find coffee and an aspirin at The Drugstore before heading on to the bank and his appointment with Miles Durig.

When he stood, however, the room tilted and it took a moment of standing with his eyes squeezed shut before the floor settled down.

When he could open them, the first thing his gaze landed on was the clock. Holy smoke, it was 9:05! He was already five minutes late.

Where the hell was his duffel bag? He needed fresh clothes. The shirt he'd worn yesterday had bloodstains all over the front and shoulders. So where was his bag, dammit? He'd left it by the bed before going back to the ranch yesterday afternoon.

Striding to the old-fashioned wardrobe, swallowing bile induced by his pounding head, Caid yanked open one of its two doors.

What the hell? Clothes hung there but, since he didn't wear skirts, they damn sure weren't his. And his bag wasn't there.

This *was* his room, right?

Yes, he'd used his key to get in. It had to be his

room. There was his hat, still hanging on the corner
of the mirror where he'd forgotten it yesterday.

Hell of a thing, a rancher forgetting his hat.

He opened the other door and was relieved to see
his jeans and bloodstained shirt hanging just where
he'd placed them, his boots side by side on the closet
floor with his socks inside them and his briefs in the
plastic bag supplied by the hotel. The bag with his
change of clothing, however, wasn't there.

Well, hell. He hated to wear dirty clothes, but he
didn't have time to track down his bag. By now,
everyone in Fort Davis knew about the accident anyway. The town was like that.

The three cowboys who'd given him a ride into
town had stopped at the sheriff's office and Caid,
hardly able to speak because his head hurt so badly,
left them to make the report while he crossed the
street to the hotel. Sheriff Elan knew where to find
him if he needed more information.

Elan's secretary would have typed up the report
first thing this morning, and by now everyone and his
dog would be discussing it anywhere in town serving
breakfast.

All of which meant Caid and Durig could have a
friendly chuckle over his bloodstained shirt without
Caid doing any unnecessary explaining, and then they
could settle down to business. No problem.

Since he'd showered last night, all he needed was
a quick shave and he was outta here. His kit was in
the bathroom so at least he knew where that was.

The bathroom, however, produced another surprise.
For one thing, there were women's toiletries all over

the counter. For another, it had the steaminess of recent use. And for a third, damn it all, his kit was nowhere to be found.

To hell with it. He didn't have time now to get huffy with the staff or find out what in blazes was going on, but they were damn sure gonna hear from him later.

Eyeing the proliferation of feminine articles, Caid used what he could. He wasn't about to use the woman's toothbrush, but he used his finger and her toothpaste, then shaved himself in record time with her pink disposable razor.

Grimacing, he put on his socks, stepped into yesterday's briefs and jeans and tugged on his boots. He was avoiding putting on his blood-soaked shirt and he knew it, but he had to wear something.

He glanced at the closet door. All he'd seen earlier was feminine clothing, but maybe her husband's things were hidden among the frills. If so, he'd borrow a shirt and explain later. For that matter, once he had the loan against the sale of his five hundred acres, he'd buy the guy a new one.

The closet held nothing but feminine disappointment. As Caid went to close the door, however, his gaze fell on a long, brown-plaid sleeve.

Hmm. Pulling out the garment, he held it up consideringly and found a woman's cotton jacket with western shirt styling. Best of all, it was huge, extra-wide shouldered and boxy, with detachable shoulder pads.

In seconds, Caid had the pads out and the shirt on. Not too bad, he thought, eyeing himself in the mirror.

The shirt was tight across the shoulders maybe and pulled a little at the chest, but it was clean.

He rolled the too-short sleeves up his forearms, snagged his hat and headed out the door. He had to shoulder his way through a lobby full of milling tourists, but finally stood on the Limpia's front porch in the bright morning sunshine.

Inhaling deeply, he grinned. Nowhere in the world had summer mornings like the Davis Mountains.

But that deep breath played hell with his delicate head, and when he went to put on his hat, he found he couldn't tolerate that either. Fortunately, the bank was just across the square from the hotel.

He wished he'd had time for a cup of coffee, but Durig would give him one.

Two hours later Caid was back at the hotel, dismayed, disbelieving and totally disturbed. No one had given him a cup of coffee.

Hell, no one had given him the time of day.

Marlie had breakfast at The Drugstore, the oddly named restaurant across from the hotel, then shopped a little before returning to her room to change into hiking boots. The state park three miles out of town had a couple of good hiking trails, she'd been told.

Driving to the park, admiring the mountain scenery and shallow, sun-sparkled Limpia Creek running beside the highway, Marlie did her best to forget the last semester of school where she was counselor at Martinez High in San Antonio. And since hiking was right up there with sweaty necks on Nicholas's hate list, she managed to keep him out of her thinking, too.

That evening when she walked into the lobby of the hotel, she was pleasantly tired and pleasantly full, having had dinner and watched the sun set at the restaurant in the park.

Ann smiled at her in greeting. "Good evening, Ms. Simms. How was your day?"

"Wonderful, thanks. This is a beautiful area."

"It is, and I say it as one who's lived here all my life. Is everything all right in your room?"

"Everything's fine. It took me a while to get used to the thin walls, but I suppose that's a minor price to pay for the hotel's history. The man in the next room kept me awake for a while with his moaning and sneezing. Sounds like he's coming down with a cold."

"I'm sorry," Ann apologized. "We've never had anyone complain about noise through the walls before. Actually, they're pretty thick. I'm even more surprised because there are two maiden ladies in the room next to yours, both probably in their seventies."

"One of the sweet things has a sneeze like a water buffalo," Marlie replied with a grin. "But once I knew where the sound came from, I had no problem sleeping through it."

She glanced around the deserted lobby. "After the crowd this morning, it's certainly quiet now. Where is everyone?"

"Out looking at the stars. Most of them won't be in till the wee hours."

"Then would anyone mind if I browse the hotel bookshelves and read for a while in the parlor?"

"Not at all. We want our guests to feel at home."

"Be right back," Marlie said as she headed up the old-fashioned staircase to pull off her hiking boots.

When Caid heard a key rattle in the lock, he turned away from the window and his perusal of the street below to deliberately step toward the center of the room.

The door swung open and a woman entered, switching on the overhead light as she did so. His roomie, apparently.

Somewhere between mid- to late-twenties, she had short tousled brown hair, a snub nose with a dusting of freckles across it, a generous mouth, and eyes that he couldn't tell the color of but which were bordered with thick lashes the same shade as her hair. She was a little on the short side perhaps, but feisty with it, he could tell.

The woman was just plain cute, he thought, the kind of cute that in a puppy would make him want to take her home.

She also completely ignored him. A strange man stood in the middle of her hotel room and she didn't so much as back up a step.

Caid rubbed a tired hand over his mouth and jaw. He'd been getting the same reaction all day…or lack of it. People he'd known all his life looked through him as if he wasn't there. He'd gotten right in Durig's face at the bank and yelled at him, but Durig hadn't even blinked.

After failing to get anyone at the bank to notice him, Caid went to The Drugstore to buy aspirin and get a cup of coffee. Though he sat at the counter right in front of the kid behind it, no one waited on him.

He finally dropped change by the cash register, took a bottle of aspirin off the shelf and left to walk to the garage where they'd towed his truck.

The vehicle was a mess and certainly not drivable, but when Caid tried to talk to Jimmy to get the low-down on repairs, the garage owner ignored him, too. An oil stain had better conversation.

Totally frustrated and even more totally bewildered, Caid used a public telephone to call the ranch. He didn't like what happened then, either.

"This is the Rollin' M," Waldo snarled, his usual way of answering the phone.

"Waldo, it's Caid. I need you to drive into town and pick me—" Caid began.

"Hello? Hello?"

"It's me," Caid said loudly. "Turn up your hearing aid, dammit. I need you to…"

But he was speaking to a dead phone. Swearing, Caid dug into his jeans for more change and punched in the ranch number again.

"Rollin' M, and buster, you better have somethin' to say. I ain't got time for this," Waldo spat.

"It's Caid. Can you hear me? I need—"

The response was an earful of profanity that would make a stevedore blush.

"It's me!" Caid yelled at the top of his lungs. "Listen up, Waldo. I need—"

Dial tone.

Defeated, Caid replaced the receiver.

Next he tried to hitch a ride to the ranch with the owners of the property adjacent to his, but the Hendersons looked right through him and turned a deaf ear.

Not knowing what else to do, he at last walked back to the hotel, snagged a cup of coffee from the complimentary carafe in the deserted lobby and climbed the stairs to his room. His head felt like a mission bell at the noon hour and all he wanted at the moment was a handful of aspirin and a bed. He'd deal with the rest later.

Well, it was later, and even after a restless nap, he still didn't know how to deal with it.

People just weren't *seeing* him. He felt like the Invisible Man, except that guy could at least be *heard*.

The woman sat down on the side of the bed opposite the one he slept in and bent to untie the laces of her hiking boots. He'd like to ask just why the heck she'd commandeered his room, but knew it was probably a lost cause. No one else today had listened to him.

She'd tugged the second boot off when she paused, still holding it in her hand, and gazed for a long moment in front of her. Then she frowned.

Following her gaze, Caid looked to see what had captured her attention. All he saw was the bed he'd spent the afternoon in. The rumpled *unmade* bed.

"Bad housekeeping," she finally muttered disapprovingly, then stripped off her socks and walked barefoot into the bathroom.

When she returned, she rummaged in a dresser drawer, came up with a clean pair of socks, picked up a bottle of lotion from the top of the bureau and sat down in the chair near the window, brushing by Caid in the process, actually touching his shirt-sleeve—well, *her* shirtsleeve—without so much as breaking stride.

What she did next had Caid groaning inwardly. The woman poured a generous dollop of lotion into her palm and proceeded to massage her cute little feet.

As soon as the peppery smell of lavender filled the room, Caid sneezed.

The woman jumped a mile.

She'd heard him! But before Caid could say anything, he sneezed again. This time, however, she paid no attention, just went on slathering lotion.

Caid sneezed again. And again.

Finally, eyes streaming, he walked to the open window behind her chair and took a deep whiff of clean, unscented mountain air. By keeping his nose pressed to the screen, he managed to keep from sneezing until she closed the bottle, put on her clean socks, picked up her key from the dresser and headed for the door, obviously not bothering with shoes.

Good. As soon as she left, Caid was finding the nearest trash receptacle. Bye-bye, lavender lotion.

But she didn't exit the room immediately. Instead, after pausing at the door, she backtracked and picked up his Stetson where he'd left it on top of the dresser.

And then she stood stock still, eyes wide and startled, her luscious mouth slightly parted as she stared in apparent amazement at his hat.

Or rather, at the blue feather he kept in the hatband.

Chapter Two

With a tentative forefinger, the woman touched the blue feather, for some reason far more interested in it than Caid's rattlesnake hatband.

"Coincidence," he heard her whisper to herself. She turned the hat over to look inside the crown.

Then, to Caid's total amazement, this cute button of a woman did an extraordinary thing.

Gazing at herself in the mirror, she put his hat on her head, where it immediately sank past her ears to cover her eyes and rest on the bridge of her nose. Grinning, she pushed it up again.

"Howdy, partner," she greeted her image in an exaggerated drawl.

Fascinated, Caid watched as she stuck her thumbs in her belt loops and set her hips to rotating in a slow swivel.

"Ah'm an ol' cowhand," she sang nasally, "from the Rio Grande, but mah…something ain't…something, and mah cheeks ain't tan…."

Smiling broadly by now, and forgetting completely to keep his nose out the window, Caid turned more fully into the room, the better to appreciate the performance of that enticingly generous derriere.

He sneezed.

The woman stopped midtwang.

Dammit, he'd swear she heard him, but instead of turning toward the sound as any normal person would, she just laughed and shook her head at the far wall, causing his Stetson to drop over her eyes again.

This time, however, she took it off, replaced it on the dresser, flipped off the light and left the room.

The show, apparently, was over.

Disappointed, Caid sighed.

And sneezed.

Well, hell. If he was sharing the room with this woman, he was damn sure getting rid of the lotion she'd just used along with anything else she had that was lavender scented.

And he *was* sharing the room. At the moment, it was the only place he had to hang his hat, literally, until he could figure out what was going on. Besides, the hotel owed him. Maybe he hadn't paid for it yet, but he'd reserved the room before they gave it to the woman. Come to that, she owed him, too.

He sneezed.

It wasn't late when Marlie slowly walked up the staircase to return to her room, but after her active day she could barely keep her eyes open. She'd read for an hour in the hotel's charmingly Victorian front parlor and now clutched the Agatha Christie mystery, planning to take it to bed with her.

Earlier, she'd asked Ann if the Hotel Limpia had any resident ghosts, but the desk clerk merely laughed, saying the only one she'd heard about, but never seen herself, mind you, was that of a soldier from the old fort.

But it wasn't a soldier Marlie thought she'd seen. For a split second, as she'd been wearing the hat with the coincidental blue feather and acting silly in front of the mirror, she thought she'd caught the vague outline of a cowboy standing near the window behind her. But then her neighbor sneezed, and of course there was nothing reflected in the mirror but herself.

The Hotel Limpia, with its antique furnishings and bygone western charm, certainly had a way of sending the imagination into overdrive, she thought, unlocking the door to her room.

Once inside, she didn't bother with the overhead light but switched on the lamp near her bed. In the dimness outside its glow, she eyed with disfavor the double bed that matched her own. Its sheets and covers were lumpy and rumpled just as they'd been this morning.

In all other respects, the hotel service was first rate, but its housekeeping staff left a lot to be desired. Marlie had meant to say something to Ann earlier and forgotten, but she was telling the desk clerk first thing in the morning. There was no excuse for an establishment of this caliber leaving beds unmade.

Gathering clean panties and her pajamas, she headed for the bathroom and a long hot bath, but after stepping out of her jeans and partially unbuttoning her shirt, she remembered the soap she'd found today in one of the shops.

Ah. The perfect end to a perfect day.

Traipsing back to the bedroom, Marlie rummaged through a couple of sacks until she found it. But just as she turned toward the bathroom again, she thought she heard a breathy whistle from next door.

It was just a whisper of sound, but for no apparent reason she suddenly became very aware of her bare legs and half-open shirt.

She grimaced. Too bad there wasn't another room available. As it was, she had a double room too big for her single self when what she needed was double walls.

All was forgiven, however, when she lowered herself into the deep bathtub. Hot water and lavender soap. Life didn't get any better.

Unless, of course, a handsome someone scrubbed her back.

Unh-huh. Cut that last thought. Nicholas wouldn't scrub her back. He'd just tell her how bad hot water and perfumed soaps were for her skin.

Forget Nicholas. And forget hats placed strategically by an interior decorator to enhance an old hotel's western decor. Forget, especially, hats with blue feathers in the hatband.

A half hour later, too pleasantly lethargic from her hot bath for even Agatha to have appeal, Marlie called it a day. Turning off the lamp, she sank into the old-fashioned bed's very modern and oh-so-comfortable mattress.

And heard a giant sneeze.

Oh. Good. Grief.

Still, if she could hear the people next door, they could surely hear her. "Don't you have anything to take for that?" she asked the wall loudly.

Silence.

One might even say *stunned* silence, it was that thick. Apparently the elderlies in the next room didn't realize how thin the walls were.

There was another sneeze, followed by a muttered, "Well, hell."

"Bless you," Marlie called out, grinning.

"You can hear me?" a voice asked diffidently.

Aha, Marlie thought. Masculine. One of the supposed maiden ladies still had some energy.

"Yes, and you really ought to take something for that cold. We'd all sleep better."

"It's not a cold," the voice replied. A husky voice, with a hint of drawl. And it didn't sound like that of an old man, either. It sounded velvety, downright sexy even, if a trifle cranky and stuffed up. One of the dears must have found herself a young stud while she was stargazing.

"It's allergies," the voice continued. "I'm allergic to your soap."

And Marlie could swear that whoever spoke was right beside her. She heard a rustling in the other bed.

With a shriek, she reached out and turned on the light.

Nothing. Even better, no one.

Sinking limply against the pillows, she sighed....

Ker-choo!

And bolted up again.

"If you'd bathe with something besides lavender soap, we'd both be happier," the voice said.

"Where *are* you?" Marlie whispered.

"In the bed opposite yours. Don't get your britches in a knot, lady. I won't hurt you."

Throwing back the covers, Marlie bolted for the door, fumbled with the lock, threw the door open and was about to slam it behind her when she realized she heard no pursuit. She paused, uncertain, but stayed poised to immediately run and/or scream, whichever was needed.

Cautiously reaching over, she flipped on the overhead light. How could she describe the intruder to the local badge if she didn't know what he looked like?

Nothing. No one. Nobody.

"Are...are you there?" she whispered into the seemingly empty room.

"I'm here."

"Where?"

"I told you. In the other bed."

The covers on the bed in question rose and fell as if they'd been given a disgusted shake. Marlie's heartbeat rose and fell with them.

"I'm...I'm going for the police," she warned, trying to keep the wobble out of her voice.

"Go ahead. If you can explain this to someone you'll be doing a hell of a lot better than I did today. And Fort Davis doesn't have police. We make do with a sheriff and a couple of deputies." *Ker-choo!*

"You've got a sneeze like an atomic blast," Marlie said dryly. "I don't think I'll have much trouble explaining things."

"Have at it," the whoever or whatever it was responded, and blew his nose.

Once the woman marched her straight-backed, swishy-bottomed little self out the door, Caid got out of bed, went to the closet and retrieved his jeans. If on the off chance someone could finally see him as well as hear him, he wanted to be decent. He wasn't holding out much hope, however.

Still, for the first time today he'd actually exchanged conversation with someone. Perhaps whatever the heck it was that had happened to him was starting to wear off.

When Marlie returned, she had Ann with her. After hearing the story, the desk clerk had talked her out of going for the sheriff.

Ann looked around the quiet room. "I don't see anything or hear anything, Ms. Simms. Are you sure you weren't dreaming?"

"I hadn't gone to sleep yet," Marlie replied shortly. "And I know what I heard. A man talked to me and he sneezed. He said he was allergic to my lavender soap.

"Hey," she called out to the seemingly empty room, feeling brave now that she had company. "Are you here?"

"I'm here," the voice answered.

"Where?"

"Standing about three feet in front of you." *Kerchoo!*

"There." Marlie turned to the desk clerk in triumph. "You heard that, didn't you? I'll bet people in the next county did, too."

But Ann merely gazed back at her in confusion. "Ms. Simms, I, uh, didn't hear anything."

"Sure you did," Marlie told the desk clerk bracingly. "That sneeze registered on the Richter scale."

But by now, even though she wasn't but a few years older, Ann's look had turned motherly. She put a comforting arm around Marlie's shoulders.

"Ms. Simms…Marlie, I think you had too much sunshine and thin mountain air today. You crawl back into bed now, honey, and I'll bring up a nice cup of herbal tea to help you sleep. You'll feel better in the morning."

Ker-choo!

"You didn't hear that?" Marlie asked in a small voice.

"No, sweetie. You get a good night's rest now and I'll bet you feel tip-top by tomorrow."

Marlie sighed. "Perhaps you're right. But I don't need any tea. Really. Thanks for coming up, though."

She walked Ann to the door and was about to shut it behind her when she noticed the bathroom trash basket sitting by the doorway in the hall. In it was her brand-new, used only once, very expensive tablet of lavender soap.

Marlie debated pointing this bit of evidence out to the desk clerk, who was wishing her good-night again, but in the end decided it probably wouldn't do much good.

After closing the door, she leaned against it to gaze accusingly into her seemingly empty bedroom. "Say something, darn it. I know you're still here."

"That makes two of us."

There was the sound a deep sigh followed by a massive *Ker-choo!*

"Oh, for goodness' sake! Do you have to keep doing that? Ghosts aren't supposed to sneeze."

"I'm not a ghost."

"Could've fooled me. What are you then?"

"Alive, for one thing. For some reason, people just can't see me, and so far the only person who can hear me is you." *Ker-choo!*

"Well aren't I just the lucky one," Marlie said nastily. "How delightful that the whole world now thinks I'm crazy."

"Not the whole world, just Ann Jergin. But she's a nice girl. She won't tell anyone."

"You know her?"

"Of course I know her. We were in the same grade all through school."

Marlie frowned in the direction of the voice, now coming from the vicinity of the other bed. In fact, the bed looked a little depressed on one side, as if someone were sitting on it.

"Who *are* you?" she asked slowly.

"I'll tell you after you shower. Lifebouy, Irish Spring, Dove. Take your pick. Any scent but lavender."

"How do I know you won't float into the shower with me? You might be anywhere for all I know."

"Lock the damn door," the voice snapped. "I can't walk through walls. I already tried."

"You could be lying."

"Yes, ma'am, I could. You're just gonna have to trust me now, aren't you?"

Why should I, Marlie wanted to ask, but didn't. A ghost with allergies seemed…trustworthy, in a bizarre sort of way.

Good grief! She *was* certifiably crazy.

But she headed for the bathroom. Just before she

closed and locked the door, however, she stuck her head out again. "Where are you?"

"Here," he replied, his tone one of long suffering, but the sound of his voice came from the bed. "Now get a move on. I'm tired, I've got a hell of a headache and I don't want to stay up all night yakking."

What a crab.

When she returned, showering in record time, the woman smelled like nothing but cleanliness. Caid had never thought of eau de clean as erotic before, but as he watched her prance across the room, then hop into bed, he had the overwhelming urge to hop into it with her.

Huh, he thought. So she had great legs. The real attraction was probably because he could talk to her. Communication could be a powerful aphrodisiac.

And strangely, though sharing a bed with the woman had strong appeal, going beyond sharing didn't seem to…suit the moment.

"What's your name?"

They'd asked the question at the same time.

"You first," the woman said. "And your story better be good, buster."

"Or what?" Caid asked, truly curious.

"I'll think of something. Don't think I won't. Now start talking."

Caid grinned. "Yes, ma'am." But his story was no laughing matter and he sobered immediately. "I'm Caid Matthews," he said. "Kincaid Matthews the Fourth, owner of the Rolling M."

"That's your feather on the dresser, isn't it?" she

said wonderingly. "I mean, your hat. Your name is inside. I thought it was part of the hotel decor."

"Only since yesterday. I forgot it when I went back to the ranch."

He heard a startled little movement in the next bed. "Oh my Lord!" the woman exclaimed. "You're the rancher who was involved in the accident. The one they took to the hospital last night."

"No, ma'am. I'm the one who ran into a tree, all right, but I never went to the hospital."

"But…but when I checked in last night, they said you'd been taken to the hospital. That's why they gave me the room."

Caid was beginning to get irritated. Whose story was this? "No, ma'am," he contradicted stubbornly. "I was right here in this bed last night."

There was a long silence. "Oh."

Though it hurt his head to do it, Caid raised up so he could look across the intervening space at the opposite bed, part of which lay in a pool of light cast by the lamp on that side of the table between them.

The woman sat against a bank of pillows, gazing into space and chewing her bottom lip, obviously thinking deeply.

"Do you remember how you got into town?" she asked at last.

Caid could tell she was keeping her tone carefully noncommittal and it riled him no end.

"Yes, I remember how I got into town. Three cowboys from the MT gave me a lift. They found my truck and I hitched a ride into town with them. But my head was killing me, so I let them talk to the sheriff and I came on here."

Uh-oh. Maybe he shouldn't have said that "killing me" part. The woman's own ideas were bad enough.

"But did you actually *talk* to them?"

She just wasn't going to leave it alone, was she? "Hell yes, I actually talked to them. Well, some. Maybe not a whole lot, but I told them I'd ride into town with them. Then I crawled into the back of their pickup and we came on to Fort Davis."

"You told them? They didn't ask? And they let an injured man ride in the night air in the *back* of the pickup? That doesn't sound strange to you?"

"Not particularly," Caid replied shortly, though come to think of it, it did seem a little harsh even for West Texas cowpokes. Nobody had even offered him a handkerchief to sop up the blood.

"Did you get a good look at your truck?" the woman then asked.

"Yeah, I saw it. What about it?"

"There was blood all over the seat."

"Doesn't mean anything. There was blood all over my head and my shirt, too. I probably had a mild concussion, but so what? I've had worse. And how do you know there was blood on the seat?"

"Your truck was the sensation of the morning, Mr. Matthews. When I had breakfast, everybody was talking about it at The Drugstore this morning, so I walked down and looked at it, too. You could see the bull's-eye in the windshield where your head hit. Why in Heaven didn't you wear your seat belt?"

Caid felt his ears turn red. "I forgot," he mumbled.

"What?"

"I forgot, dammit, just like I forgot my hat and just

like I forgot the blasted papers in the first place. I've had a lot on my mind lately.''

There was another long silence.

''Something else was being talked about in the restaurant this morning, Mr. Matthews,'' she said at last.

''Caid.''

''Um, Caid. People were talking about the latest news from the hospital after the ambulance took you to the emergency room. They said…''

She paused, and Caid had a feeling he wasn't going to like what came next.

''They said, um, Caid, that you were…on life support.''

It was Caid's turn to be silent for a long moment. ''Yeah?''

''Yeah.''

''Well, hell. All I know is, I'm not in the hospital, I'm sitting right here on this bed talking to you, and the only thing wrong with me is a humdinger of a headache.''

And then she just had to say it. ''But no one can see you or hear you.''

''You can.''

''I can hear you, but I can't see you. Mr. Matthews…Caid…I'm sorry to have to say this, but I— I think you died. Life support keeps the body going, but it doesn't necessarily keep the spirit going.''

''Bull hockey. I'd know it if I was dead. I'd have seen the light or something. And why the heck would I stick around town when I could go to Paradise?''

''Maybe Paradise isn't an option. Or maybe you just don't know you're dead. I mean, isn't that kind of what a ghost is, someone who doesn't understand that they're dead so they refuse to go to the other side? That's why they do exorcisms, isn't it?''

"Exorcisms! Lady, are you crazy?'' Caid sat straight up in bed, then had to grab his ears to keep his head from bouncing off. Hell, if he was a ghost he wouldn't have this damn headache. And what did she mean, maybe Paradise wasn't an option?

By now, Marlie was near tears. There was no easy way to tell someone they were dead and this man just kept *arguing* with her.

"My name is Marlie,'' she said, "and I'm not the one who's crazy here. Everyone can hear and see me just fine, thank you very much. It's you who can't seem to get with the program. If you'd just go on to the other side like you're supposed to, you wouldn't have this problem.''

"Marlie what?''

"Simms,'' she said, and sniffed.

"Marlie Simms, are you crying?''

The voice from the other bed sounded very gentle. She could have liked this man, Marlie thought. When he wasn't being stubborn.

"I'm s-sorry you're dead,'' she said wetly.

She could almost feel his instant withdrawal.

"I'm not dead. Now turn out the light and let's get some sleep. I'm tired of arguing. My head feels like a Chinese gong at prayer time and I'm out of aspirin.''

Marlie blinked. "You've been taking aspirin?''

"While I had it, but I can't say it's done much good.''

"There's medication stronger than aspirin,'' she

said tentatively. "I, um, have some in my purse. I'll give you a couple of tablets, if you like."

"Appreciate it."

Throwing back the covers, she left the bed to get her purse, returning to sit on the edge to rummage through the bag in the lamplight. Naturally the ibuprofen was on the bottom so that she had to take out a few things.

"Say. Are you going to eat that candy bar?"

Startled, she looked over at the bed next to hers that appeared empty, yet was so very full of pure unadulterated male. How she knew that last she wasn't quite certain, except that a picture had begun to form in her mind from the moment she'd picked up his hat.

"You're...you're *hungry?*"

"Haven't eaten a bite all day. When I tried to order a meal, no one would listen to me."

"Here, take it," Marlie said immediately. But with no hand to give it to, she placed the chocolate bar on the far side of the bedside table. It immediately disappeared.

"I also have a couple of packages of crackers, and a granola bar," she added, placing them, too, on the nightstand.

She heard the rustle of paper wrappings and a crumbly, "Thanks," as if Caid was talking with his mouth full. In seconds, the crackers and granola bar vanished. Discarded wrappers appeared in the trash basket under the night table.

It was all very disconcerting, but not nearly as disconcerting as seeing the water carafe disappear and water slowly fill one of the glasses left for guests at their bedside. When the carafe reappeared and the glass disappeared, Marlie hurriedly placed two pain relievers within reach. *Poof.* They, too, were gone.

"Um, Caid," Marlie said slowly, "I don't suppose you'd consider haunting another room?"

"Not on your life. I reserved for two nights, I'm staying two nights. It's thanks to me that you have the room at all."

"I was afraid you'd say that." Marlie sighed, and switched off the lamp.

"And I'm *not* dead."

She let him have the last word, mainly because she was too startled to speak. Just as she plunged the room into darkness, she thought she'd seen the blurry outline of a dark head on the pillow of the other bed.

Turning over, she closed her eyes.

Nah, couldn't be.

Chapter Three

Bright sunlight and a piercing whistle from somewhere outside caused Caid to sit straight up in bed.
Lordy, he hadn't slept this late in years. His head still
hurt, but not with the splitting agony of the day before.

He yawned and leisurely scratched his bare chest,
then threw back the covers and left the bed. First thing
on the agenda today was figuring out how to get
breakfast or he'd be down to eating his boots.

But before he headed to the closet for his jeans—
his dirty jeans—he paused a moment to gaze at the
woman who still slept peacefully in the other bed.

Marlie Simms. A dumpling of a woman, just the
right size to fill a man's arms, he'd bet. Too bad she
also had the look of a woman who didn't take that
kind of thing lightly. Because lightly was the only
thing Caid was interested in anymore.

The last time he'd taken a woman seriously, she'd

taken him to the cleaners in the divorce courts—the main reason the Rolling M was in the financial crisis it was in right now.

Still, he had to admit Marlie had been pretty decent about letting a strange man share her hotel room, even if only because she thought he was a ghost.

She stirred and Caid backed up a step before he remembered that she couldn't see him. So he lingered, fascinated by the way the woman stretched all over before she opened her eyes. Her two arms went over her head in a long slow reach for the ceiling and she inhaled deeply.

Then—and by now, Caid had stopped breathing completely—her whole body undulated in one long…luxurious…sensuous…writhe.

His throat went dry.

Then her mouth parted in a dainty kitten of a yawn, and she slowly opened her eyes….

And screamed at the top of her lungs, nearly giving him a heart attack.

She was fumbling frantically at the bedside phone only to drop the receiver between the nightstand and the bed before he came to his senses.

"What is it?" he managed to gasp, by now on his knees groping under the bed in an effort to retrieve the receiver for her. "Are you having a seizure? What?"

"You! Who… How…"

Caid, finally finding the phone, handed it to her and sat back on his butt, their faces now at a level.

"Who the heck are you and get the heck out of my room!" she finally managed to get out.

Well, hell. They were back to this.

"Marlie," Caid said patiently, "I told you last night who I am. Remember?" He was the one with the head wound here.

"Caid?" Her tone sounded disbelieving.

"Yeah. Caid Matthews."

She stared him right in the eye as he squatted by her bed. Her eyes were a pale silvery gray, he noted, and looked mad as bedamned.

"Caid Matthews," she screeched, setting his ears to ringing and escalating his headache up a notch, "you're naked as a jaybird! Get out of my room!" and she threw a pillow at him.

But Caid didn't move. "You can *see* me?"

And Marlie finally seemed to grasp the importance of the moment. She blinked in startlement, then slowly, wickedly grinned. "Yes, Caid, I can *definitely* see you."

"Thank God." Leaning forward, Caid bussed her on the cheek, stood and all in the same movement, tossed the pillow in the air, pumped a triumphant fist and caught it when it came down.

Marlie tried to keep her gaze on the flying pillow, or on Caid's exuberant face. She really did.

But she really couldn't.

From sheer self-preservation, she reached behind her and threw the other pillow at him, hitting him right in the midsection. Fortunately, it was a large pillow.

"Don't you have any clothes?" she asked.

"Clothes?"

Comprehension dawned. "Oh. Clothes."

He clutched the pillow to him strategically, trying

to look nonchalant as only a man with red ears can. "Well, don't just sit there. Close your eyes."

Marlie obligingly closed her eyes, opening them as soon as she heard the wardrobe door open, the better to admire Caid's rock-hard little rear as he took his jeans off a hanger. As soon as he stepped into his pants and turned around, she snapped them shut again.

"You don't fool me, Cutes. You were peeking."

"Was not." Well, not actually *peeking*. Her eyes had been wide open.

"So, like what you saw?"

She tried her best to look righteously indignant. "I didn't see a thing."

"Huh."

Once Caid left for the bathroom, Marlie hopped out of bed to get her pillows, then jumped back in again and leaned against them. She didn't want to get up just yet.

For one thing, the two of them milling around the room in states of semidress was just a little intimate for her peace of mind. It was far easier to deal with this cowboy's disembodied spirit than it was his materialized substance. And what a substance!

But Caid was definitely on his way to somewhere and once he left the room, she'd get up herself. In the meantime, she'd savor the mental image of the tightest tush she'd seen in a long time.

When he emerged from the bathroom, Caid's hair was damp and curled the least bit, and Marlie took a couple of seconds to get a good look at his face, the rest of his anatomy being already etched in her mind.

It was a good face, she thought, angles and planes

in all the right places, a nose just a trifle large and definitely arrogant, eyes the color of pine needles.

One eye, however, had a dilly of a shiner, with its bruise taking up half of Caid's smooth cheek below and reaching into his hairline above. On the same side, his forehead bore a big knot topped with an ugly-looking gash.

He sat down in a nearby chair to pull on his boots. "Damn, I hate dirty socks," he muttered. "Do you have any idea where my bag is?"

"Ann took it when she gave me the room."

He sighed. "I'll get it later. And I need my kit. It's hell shaving with a pink razor."

"You used my razor! Yuck! You better not have used my toothbrush."

"Eww. I only used your toothpaste." Caid stood and stamped his feet into his boots, then went to the closet and pulled out a shirt.

"Hey, that's mine. You can't wear a woman's jacket. Besides, it'll never fit you."

"Sorry, darlin'. I wore it yesterday. It's too big to fit a little scrap like you, anyway, even as a jacket."

He pulled on the garment in question and began buttoning it, and her pseudo-oversized shirt-cum-jacket transformed itself into a definitely masculine article of clothing. A little tight across Caid's broad shoulders perhaps, but Marlie had to admit the "shirt" looked far better on him than it did her.

"I'll buy you a new one," he was saying, "as soon as I get everything straightened out this morning." He grimaced. "My own is full of blood and I threw it out. Right now, though, I'm going to breakfast. Want me to bring you some coffee?"

Hard to believe she'd first laid eyes on this man not twenty minutes ago, Marlie thought. Here he was, wearing her clothes and offering to fetch her coffee.

"Uh, no thanks. I'll be going to breakfast myself in a few minutes. I have to say, though, that you seem pretty certain of yourself for a man who was a ghost yesterday."

"Well, it's over, Cutes. You see me." Caid glanced at himself in the mirror. "I see me. 'Course, I saw myself yesterday, too, but that doesn't mean anything. And I feel good. My head doesn't hurt much and I had a good night's sleep. So whatever it was, it's gone. If you'll make it snappy and get on over to The Drugstore, I'll buy you breakfast."

With a cocky wink and a "See you there," he was out the door and gone.

Marlie shook her head. Nothing about this situation made sense and she wasn't at all certain that it was as over as Caid believed. Yes, she could hear him. But she'd also been able to hear him yesterday when no one else could. And today she could see him, and what a sight he was. She could feel him, too.

She reached up to touch the cheek that Caid had kissed. Oh, she could definitely feel him. Soft lips, a little rough stubble. Her face still tingled.

But none of that explained the riddle of how everyone in town, except Caid, knew he was in the hospital, fighting for his life.

Marlie sighed. The question was, did Kincaid Matthews have any life left to fight for? It was a scientific fact that no one could be in two places at once. No one alive, that was.

And he had the blue feather. Had Grammie's Great

Ones decided she was such a lost cause that the only man she could have was a ghost? Still, she'd warned her grandmother that she wasn't buying, only playing. And since Gram hadn't actually *given* her the feather, perhaps this situation fit the latter category.

She was standing at the dresser mirror, putting on her lipstick, when a key rattled in the door and Caid came in. He'd been gone exactly seventeen and a half minutes.

Throwing himself into the same chair where he'd so cheerfully pulled on his boots, he now stared gloomily down at their dusty toes.

"Well, hell," he said. "No one could see me. Or hear me. I might as well have been invisible. Hell, I *am* invisible."

He threw his Stetson across the room so that it landed on the bed upside down. "And I'm *hungry!* How can a ghost be hungry, dammit? Tell me that."

Though he glared at Marlie, he knew he was being unfair to ask her for answers. But he knew, too, that he had to ask *somebody.*

Forking his fingers through his hair, he hit a particularly sensitive bruise and winced. "For that matter, how the *hell* can it have a headache?"

She didn't answer. Couldn't answer, he thought bitterly. No one could.

But she left her place at the mirror to come over and kneel in front of him, and take one of his hands.

He noticed, however, that she hesitated the least bit before her fingers closed around his, and that slight hesitation only enraged him further.

But as much as he wanted to snatch his hand away, his very soul needed the human contact.

He could *feel* Marlie, dammit, feel her small warm hand over his own tightly clenched fist. And he could *smell* her, an odor of soap and cosmetics, and a crisp spicy something that was unique only to her. Everything about this woman filled his senses.

And now her silvery gray eyes were gazing up at him with commiseration. *She* could see him. Why couldn't everyone else?

"I'm sorry, Caid," she said, and he could tell that she really was. "I wish I had answers for you."

He'd opened his mouth to say something caustic when his stomach growled audibly.

Marlie grinned. "How about if I bring *you* breakfast?"

"How about if I go with you?"

Enough of feeling sorry for himself. Pulling her up with him, Caid stood. He had to *do* something. "Maybe whatever there is that allows you to see me will rub off on somebody else."

He fought the urge to cling to the hand still in his, but let it go to walk to the bed and retrieve his hat.

The Drugstore was popular with locals and tourists alike, and it took them a moment to locate a table toward the back of the crowded noisy room.

Threading their way through the mass of tables and people, Caid spoke to several men he knew, but not one of them so much as glanced his way or replied.

At the moment, however, he was beyond caring. The smell of bacon, eggs and coffee was about to do him in.

"Order plenty," he told Marlie when Linda Frick,

the teenage daughter of one of Caid's oldest friends handed only Marlie a menu.

"Coffee?" Linda asked brightly.

Marlie smiled at her. "Yes, please."

"Two," Caid said.

"Er, make that two coffees."

Linda looked startled for a moment, then grinned. "Oh, someone's still coming. Sure thing. Anything else?"

"A large orange juice and a glass of milk," Caid said.

This time when Marlie repeated the order, Linda didn't bat an eye. "Be right back," she said cheerfully.

And she was, placing one steaming mug in front of Marlie and one in front of Caid. She looked a little indecisive about where to place the milk and orange juice, but finally put them both in the middle of the table.

"Ready to order?"

Marlie ordered scrambled eggs and toast for herself, and under his direction, ordered a breakfast steak, a Spanish omelette, hash browns, grits, bacon, sausage, biscuits and gravy *and* toast for Caid.

Linda's eyebrows went up. "Your friend likes to eat," she commented.

"Apparently," Marlie said, "and he doesn't pay much attention to his cholesterol, either." She looked meaningfully at Caid.

"Cholesterol is the least of my problems," Caid answered. "I dandled our waitress here on my knee."

Marlie sighed. "Sorry."

"Oh, don't worry about it," Linda replied breezily,

smiling at her. "My dad eats like that, too." And she hurried off to turn in their order.

Once food was on the table, Caid plowed into it with a vengeance. He had impeccable manners, Marlie noticed, but the food in front of him disappeared like magic. Literally like magic if anyone but herself was watching, she supposed. But in the crowded restaurant, where every table was full, no one gave them any special attention.

Linda returned just as they both were finishing up. "More coffee?"

Caid, his mouth full of biscuit and gravy, nodded toward his empty cup.

"Please," Marlie said.

Linda poured coffee for her and was about to leave again, when Marlie added, "And for my, ah, friend, too, please."

"Oh. Sorry. Thought he'd left already."

"No, he…he's in the men's room."

After Linda poured Caid's coffee, she placed their bill near his side of the table. "Ya'll can pay me at the register when you're ready to leave. Take your time, though."

Which said a lot for small town hospitality, Marlie thought, considering how crowded the place was.

"I'll just get these dirty dishes out of your way," Linda said, and began clearing the table.

The toe of Caid's boot connected with Marlie's ankle.

She jumped, and glared across the table at him. "What did you do that for?"

"I still have some biscuit," he told Marlie, scowling, and nodded at his plate where a half-eaten biscuit covered in white gravy still sat, waiting for his attention.

"Well, you didn't have to kick me," Marlie told him.

Linda stared at her in embarrassed confusion. "Oh, ma'am. I'm so sorry. I didn't mean to, honest."

It was Marlie's turn to be confused, until she remembered that Linda had no idea who she'd actually been talking to.

"No, not you, sweetie. Someone passed too close to the table and kicked me. No harm done," and she smiled for all she was worth. The girl was definitely getting a good tip.

"Leave those dishes," she added, nodding toward Caid's side of the table. "My, uh, friend isn't finished."

"Sure," Linda said, but she eyed Marlie warily.

When she left—hurriedly—Marlie glared at Caid. "Add our waitress to the list of people now thinking I'm crazy."

Caid speared his last bite of biscuit and used it to mop up the last bit of gravy. "She was taking my food. How else was I supposed to stop her? She sure couldn't hear me."

He had a point. Invisibility must be awful for him.

Finally pushing aside his shining plate, Caid grinned with satisfaction and picked up his coffee cup. "That was good. I think I'll live."

At her look, however, the grin slipped. "Don't say it. I was joking."

Digging into his jeans, he pulled out a wad of bills. "This ought to cover it."

"I can pay for my own," Marlie said, already opening her wallet.

Caid reached over and lightly grasped her arm. "When I eat with a lady, I pay," he said quietly, but his gaze dared her.

Marlie sighed and shook her head. She'd known a few true cowboys in her day and they were all alike. Heartbreakers every one, but old-fashioned to the bone.

It was useless to argue. "Thank you."

"You'll have to handle the money at the register, though. If Linda sees dollars appear out of thin air, she'll swallow her bubblegum. But do me a favor, will you?"

"Depends," Marlie replied, gathering her purse, Caid's money and the bill.

"Ask her how I'm doing."

She looked up, and her heart did a little skip. Caid's face wore no expression.

"All right."

It was so hard to remember the man beside her was in spirit only. He just seemed so normal, so vital.

So *male*. Not in the least vaporish.

It took a couple of minutes for Linda to make her way to the register and when she saw Marlie standing in front of it, she grinned, evidently over her momentary consternation.

"Left you the check, did he?" she teased. "Bummer."

Marlie shrugged and laughed. "It's his money. Uh, Linda, have you heard how Mr. Matthews is doing?"

"Caid Matthews? I don't think I've heard anything today."

"I heard Caid's still in a coma," a man wearing bib overalls and sitting at the counter nearby volunteered. "They say he's gonna be paralyzed from the neck down."

"Real shame," someone else offered. "But I hear when he wakes up, they're expectin' brain damage. Might be a vegetable."

"Oh, dear God," Marlie breathed. Beside her, she heard Caid's sharp intake of breath.

"It's a shame, all right," the first man said. "A friend of my brother-in-law had a head wound just like ol' Caid's. They had to put him in a home. Never did get right."

"Same thing happened to my cousin's kid," another man offered. "He's been in a wheelchair for twenty years. But he's sharp as a tack. Went on and got a college degree an' all. Just goes to show."

A woman spoke up, ready to add her story to the pot, "A friend of mine…" but by now Marlie had heard enough.

When she turned to ask Caid if he had, too, he was gone.

Snatching up the receipt, she threw a quick smile at Linda, who was gazing at the restaurant's screen doors with her mouth open.

"Wind," the girl said faintly and gave her head a little shake.

Once on the sidewalk, Marlie gazed frantically around. The street was busy and the sidewalk crowded with tourists. But Marlie didn't see Caid anywhere.

And then she did, far down the sidewalk and walking fast. She hurried after him.

"Caid," she shouted. A couple of people turned around but not the one she wanted. "Caid!" And she started running.

Finally, he stopped and slowly turned. His face was ashen beneath its bruises, she saw, but his eyes were defiant as ever.

"I'm not dead," he said. "I'm not paralyzed and I'm not brain damaged. I don't know what's wrong with me, but I do know it's not…that."

"Where are you going?"

"Nowhere. Just walking. Where the hell can I go that anyone will see me? Now *that's* my problem."

"Do you mind if I walk with you?"

He sighed. "C'mon and I'll show you the town."

Caid led her off the main drag and they meandered down the back streets, past houses and churches old and modern, rich and poor, all jumbled together. But Marlie didn't ask Caid any questions about them and he didn't volunteer any information.

They walked without speaking, the sun growing hot on their shoulders until Caid finally stopped in the shade of an apricot tree.

Without asking permission, he picked Marlie up and set her atop a low rock wall that formed a fence around a two-story Victorian house. Then he hoisted himself up beside her.

"Marlie," he said, after a long moment. "Would you take me home?"

"Home?"

"To the Rolling M. Maybe there I can get myself back again. I know it's a long drive, but I'll buy your gas. Not many tourists get to see a real working ranch up close," he added coaxingly.

"Oooh, really! Can I pat your horse? Maybe see a real live cow?"

He chuckled. "You're not impressed, I can tell."

"I'm from San Antonio, Cowboy. Impress me with something else."

"Well, they don't have the Davis Mountains in San Antonio, and they don't have the Rolling M, the prettiest little mountain ranch in the state."

"Hmm, a definite selling point. When do you want to leave?"

"As soon as possible or immediately, whichever is more convenient."

Marlie hopped off the low wall. "Now seems a good time, if you're not in any hurry."

It was, as Caid said, a long drive. After driving almost an hour deep into the Davis Mountains, Marlie was glad her vehicle was an SUV once they left the pavement and pulled onto the ranch property itself.

He was wrong about one thing, however. The Rolling M wasn't "a pretty little mountain ranch."

Pretty, yes. Beautiful, in fact. But little? Not in Marlie's definition of the word. She spent a good forty-five minutes carefully negotiating inclines and declines, ruts, rocks and a couple of creek bottoms before the ranch's big house came into view.

Killing the motor with a heartfelt sigh of relief, she stiffly pried her white-knuckled fingers from the steering wheel. "I'll bet you don't have any trouble with burglars."

"Hmm?" Caid's attention was clearly elsewhere. "Waldo's not here," he said.

"Who?"

"Waldo, my foreman. He shouldn't be off the ranch when I'm gone."

"Perhaps he's at the hospital," Marlie said gently. "Surely there's someone else to watch things here." Lord knew the place was big enough for a small army.

"No, there's just me and Waldo. I let the other hands go after the spring gather."

A dog came racing toward them, barking for all it was worth, and Caid left the car. "Hey, Dynamite, we're friendly," he said, laughing, and squatted to fondle the dog's ears.

Marlie, too, left the SUV, smiling as the blue heeler stretched his neck in ecstasy under Caid's massaging fingers. Clearly besotted with his owner, Dynamite reached up and slurped a wet tongue over the cowboy's face, his stubby tail wagging so hard his hindquarters shook with it.

Obviously the dog had no trouble seeing or hearing Caid.

Perhaps Caid was right, Marlie thought. Perhaps on the ranch, a place that was his and no other's, he could somehow get himself back again.

No others? Was she sure? A wife, perhaps? Children?

But as soon as she realized where her thoughts were headed, she killed them immediately.

In spite of their matching blue feathers, she was through with men, she reminded herself, and turned her face up to silently remind the Great Ones of it, too.

She especially didn't want a man up to his ears in trouble.

Getting involved with other people and their unfix-able problems had almost cost her her job. It had cer-tainly cost her a fiancé. Not again, she vowed.

So what if everything inside her wanted to know all about Caid Matthews? Wanted to "fix" this strange situation he was in? She couldn't. End of in-volvement.

Swallowing the lump in her throat at seeing the gratification written all over Caid's face that his dog knew him, she turned her attention to the huge log house behind them.

"You have a beautiful home," she said.

Caid stood. "Thanks. My dad built it for my mother for their twenty-fifth wedding anniversary. It's her design. Too bad she didn't live to see it finished."

"I'm sorry."

"Yeah. Me, too. Would you like to come inside? I'll rustle up some lunch."

Passing through a wide front porch that went on to wrap around one corner of the house, he opened the front door for her.

It wasn't locked, Marlie noted.

The inside of the house was open and airy, fur-nished with a mix of traditional and modern, ranch-style and urban. A home clearly for living, not im-pressing.

It was also dusty, and its beautiful hardwood floors badly scuffed in places.

So maybe there's not a wife, Marlie thought.

But the kitchen was spotlessly clean. Caid went to the refrigerator and pulled out sandwich meat, lettuce, tomato, onion, cheese—everything for a large, man-size sandwich on whole wheat bread.

He ate three of them to Marlie's one. They talked a bit, sitting at the kitchen table, about the weather and about the latest political scandal, about the growth of the area and its possible effect on the water table.

They did not talk about themselves or each other. Or Caid's difficulty in rationalizing who he was as opposed to who it was lying in the hospital.

It was a pleasant meal. Caid was a pleasant man.

If he was a man.

Afterwards, he walked her back to the SUV and they stood for a moment in the afternoon sunshine, a canyon wren trilling down the scale somewhere in the building-size boulders scattered around them.

"Thanks for bringing me home, Marlie."

She smiled around the stupid lump in her throat. "My pleasure." Then, in spite of herself, she added, "You're sure you'll be all right now?"

"I'm sure."

He cupped her face. "You're a sweetheart," he said. "I wish things were different." And he kissed her.

Not on the cheek.

Marlie left with the taste of him still on her lips, the feel of his warm work-roughened hands against her cheeks, the zing still racing through her blood at his touch, his taste, his essence.

Essence, she thought, pulling herself together sharply. That's all Caid Matthews was. The one she'd just left, anyway. The real man was in a coma at the Brewster County Memorial Hospital, which made the man who'd kissed her an illusion. Worse, he was an illusion with a huge problem.

She was not, repeat not, poking her nose into anyone else's life again. *Life* being an iffy word choice here.

Aside from his gorgeous butt, his sexy velvety drawl and a kiss that ought to be banned as an illegal weapon, Caid Matthews, this one anyway, was only a dream.

Literally.

Time to wake up and smell the coffee.

Chapter Four

When Marlie returned to the Hotel Limpia, she found her room clean and orderly. Both beds neatly made. No evidence of anyone having used the room but herself.

So why did she feel so disappointed?

Turning on her heel, she walked right back out the door. There was a small art gallery down the street. She would check it out.

It didn't take long to view a dozen paintings of cattle and working cowboys, all against a backdrop of dry range and rugged mountains. When, on closer inspection, one of the cowboys, frozen in time riding hell for leather after a racing steer, appeared to have a tiny blue something in the area of his hatband, Marlie decided it was time to leave.

The fact that Caid had a blue feather that matched her own was making her more and more nervous. Gram might not have bought Marlie's feather, but she'd pointed it out as a sign from the Great Ones.

And this sign was a doozy. For one thing, the man pointed out for Marlie's possible pleasure wasn't quite…a man.

Manly, yes. Hmm-*hmm!* But surely even the Great Ones wouldn't hook Marlie up with a ghost.

Not that Marlie was planning on hooking up with anybody, at least not on a permanent basis. However, as she'd told her grandmother, she wasn't at all averse to playing a little while she was on vacation.

The fact remained, though, that blue feather or not, Caid Matthews was in no position to play at the moment, whatever shape he was in.

It was all very disappointing. That was it. *Disappointment* was the reason the sparkle had gone out of the day, leaving Marlie not quite sure what to do with the rest of it.

Touring the old fort was out; it was too late in the day to give it the time it deserved. She could go to the observatory tonight for the weekly star party, but it looked to be clouding over. There was a doll museum, but she'd driven a lot today and didn't feel like getting back behind the wheel.

Besides, dolls reminded her of Nicholas, who'd wanted to wait five or ten years to have children. Five or ten *years?* Marlie, putting her own dreams aside, had agreed.

She'd been such a twit.

Well, she was a twit no more. Rain on Nicholas. And rain on blue feathers, too. She would have a good time in Fort Davis if it killed her.

It almost did. Deep in thought, she stepped out between two parked cars to cross the street and was nearly run down by a dilapidated old pickup going a spanking ten miles an hour.

Marlie leaped back, brakes squealed…probably for the first time in decades…and the truck came to a shuddering halt. In seconds, Marlie had a bandy-legged old cowboy, who had surely shaken hands with Methuselah, glaring up at her and cussing for all he was worth.

"Ain't I got enough on my plate without you trying to tear up the front end of my pickup?" he snarled. "Gol dang it, missy. Ain't you got no sense?"

And Marlie, who rarely cried but had been close to it all day, burst into tears. "You're right. You're absolutely right. It was all my fault. I'm so sorry. I didn't look where I was going."

She sniveled and hiccuped and swiped at her eyes, and the next thing she knew, the elderly cowboy had taken a completely different tack.

"Now, missy. Don't you go blamin' yourself like that. I should'na been drivin' so fast, speedin' like I was when there's tourists about. You city folk cain't he'p it you got short-changed at the sense factory." He patted her arm consolingly.

Marlie laughed, fished in her pocket for a tissue, and blew her nose.

"You're absolutely right, sir. I seem to have no sense whatsoever these days. You weren't driving fast at all. I just wasn't watching where I was going."

"I ain't a sir," the old cowboy growled. "I'm Waldo Curtis with the Rollin' M. An' if I say it wadn't your fault, it wadn't your fault."

"The Rolling M? You work for Mr. Matthews?"

"Caid Matthews. That's what I said." Waldo frowned and jerked his ancient hat further down his head.

Marlie suspected it was a gesture of worry. "How is he?" she asked gently.

"The doc says he's holdin' his own, whatever that means," Waldo replied tersely. "You know Caid, do ya?"

"Well, I, um. They gave me his room at the hotel. Mr. Curtis…er, Waldo," she corrected herself when he scowled, "I was about to have a cup of coffee at the sandwich shop across the street. Would you care to join me?"

When Waldo hesitated, she tacked on, "I'd appreciate the company. I'm still a little shaky, you know"

He patted her arm again. "Now, missy. You just pull yourself together. We'll get some coffee in you and you'll be just fine, I gar-an-tee."

Waldo wasn't too impressed with Raspberry Mocha, the flavor of the day, but with three heaping spoons of sugar he managed to drink it with no more than a disgusted grimace.

"Have you worked for Caid long?" Marlie asked tentatively.

"All his life. Worked for his daddy, now work for the son. He's a good boy. Know him well, do ya?"

"I, uh…"

Waldo stared at her suspiciously. "Might as well spit it out, missy. You ain't no good atall at lyin'."

No, Marlie thought. She wasn't. "My name's Marlie Simms," she said. "And I've had a very weird experience."

*   *   *

It felt so good to finally be able to tell someone about it. Waldo listened without comment, his face wearing no expression, as Marlie poured out her story about discovering Caid in her hotel room, being able to hear him but not being able to see him. Then being able to hear *and* see him, but no one else being able to. And finally about taking him back to the Rolling M.

"Am I crazy?" she asked at last.

"Yes, ma'am, I think you are," Waldo replied. "Caid ain't dead. And gol durn it, he ain't dyin' neither!" the old man added fiercely. "An' I don't appreciate you sayin' he is."

Marlie swallowed a lump in her throat. "I—I'm sorry. I don't want him to die, either," she said in a small voice. "He...he seemed a very nice man."

"Course he is."

Waldo found a keen interest in the sugar bowl. "The boy's had a lotta worries lately, though," he said slowly, not taking his eyes off it. "Fact is, Caid's got a hard head. It's a Matthews' trait. I can tell you he ain't one to let some piddly little tree get the better of him."

He shot a quick glance at Marlie before returning his gaze to the tabletop. "Or to let some hospital keep him corralled in a room either, even if it does have him hooked up to needles and machines and such."

The defenseless sugar bowl found itself on the receiving end of a scowl that would fell a marine battalion.

"I been kinda thinkin'," he told it slowly, his voice dropping, "that Caid's prob'ly in this here coma just

to get away from things for a while. Restin', you
know. Maybe visitin' the hotel.''

Amazed, Marlie leaned back in her chair and stared
across the table at the old cowboy, who still refused
to meet her eye.

What Waldo was hinting at, she realized, was that
he would believe her preposterous story if she in turn
would believe his preposterous supposition that
Caid's coma was merely some sort of mental vacation, that soon the boss of the Rolling M would come
home and work his ranch again just like always.

And why should she not believe it? Marlie asked
herself. After all, she knew her story was true, so who
was to say Waldo's wishful thinking was not?

''I think you're probably right,'' she said.

Waldo looked up and their eyes locked, two un-
likely conspirators who believed utterly in what could
not possibly be.

After Waldo left, Marlie ordered a sandwich to go
and walked back to the hotel. It was late afternoon by
this time. Everyone seemed to be somewhere; having
dinner perhaps. She had the main drag to herself, and
once back at the hotel found the lobby deserted as well.

Slowly she walked up the stairway, not in the mood
to appreciate the hotel's history tonight. At the door of
her room, she paused for a moment before opening it.

But the room was just as she left it.

After a hot bath—too bad she didn't have her
lavender soap anymore—she climbed into her pajamas, unwrapped her sandwich and ate it in bed as she
watched a rerun of *Friends*.

It didn't take long to enjoy all the television she

could stand. Turning out the light, she called it a day. The dark room was quiet, peaceful.

No one sneezed.

Feeling sunshine on her face, Marlie sighed blissfully, lifted her arms in a languorous stretch, opened her mouth to yawn and opened her eyes to half-mast.

"I love watching you wake up."

A shriek doesn't come easy in the middle of a full-blown yawn. Marlie strangled on a choking gasp before finally having air enough to glare at the man sitting casually on the side of the opposite bed.

"Sorry to scare you," Caid said.

"Try knocking next time," she replied, forcing herself to keep her ferocious frown. She'd never been so glad to see anyone in her life. "What are you doing here? I thought I took you home."

"You did. Waldo brought me back this morning."

Giving up on the frown, Marlie sat forward to wrap her arms around her knees and ask curiously, "Could he see you?"

"No, but he seemed to know I was there. He'd talk to me, but when I answered, he didn't hear me. It drove us both nuts, I think, and I scared him pretty badly a couple of times."

Caid's elbows rested on the top of his thighs and he slowly twirled his hat between his knees. The blue feather arced across and disappeared repeatedly.

Like a miniature comet, Marlie thought as she watched it. The ones often mistaken for a shooting star. Should she make a wish, even knowing it wasn't the real thing?

"He told me he was going to the hospital this

morning," Caid continued. "Talked real loud, like he thought I couldn't hear him, either." He, too, watched his hat circle within his two hands.

"All I seemed to get accomplished was make Waldo and Dynamite nervous, so I packed a bag and when he pulled out, I hopped in the back of the truck. Maybe he knew I was there because when we passed in front of the hotel, he slowed to a stop and just sat there for a couple of minutes, giving me time to get out. I came on up to the room. Still have my key, you know."

"You're sure you didn't walk through the wall?" Marlie asked, just to tease him a bit. She hated the lost look on his face.

And was rewarded when he looked up at her and grinned. "No, ma'am. If I could walk through walls, I'd have joined you in the shower the other night. You've got the prettiest legs I've ever seen."

"Hah!" Marlie replied, pretending to be insulted, but inside she was gratified. She *did* have good legs. Nicholas had never mentioned them.

Actually, all that Nicholas had mentioned was her overgenerous butt. He'd kindly recommended exercises and given her a copy of Dr. Atkins's book for Christmas.

What had she ever seen in the jerk anyway? Even if he was a trifle vague, Caid Matthews was twice the man Nicholas was.

The thought brought Marlie up short. She'd fallen hard for Nicholas, deliberately overlooking his less-than-stellar moments. And the rat had run when it looked for a bit as if Marlie's employment ship was sinking.

If she wasn't extremely careful, she was going to fall hard for Caid Matthews and his blue feather, too. Time to get real. Very real.

"Why did you come back here particularly?" she asked abruptly.

"Because it gets damn lonesome not having anybody to talk to," Caid replied. "Until this situation gets straightened out, however the hell it straightens out, I thought maybe you wouldn't mind if I hung out with you for a while. Show you around and things."

Marlie sat up very straight. "What *things?*"

"Hell, Marlie. I don't know. Be your roommate till I can figure out what to do. Be your friend while you're here."

She threw a pillow at him. It wasn't a friendly throw.

Before she could fire another one, Caid raised both hands. "Hey, cut it out! I surrender, already. I said roommate, not bedmate. And I said friend, not boyfriend."

"I'm not interested in messing around," Marlie said dangerously.

"Believe me, Cutes, I'm not either. But we can be pals, can't we? There's bound to be a connection somewhere, you know, because you're the only one who can see and hear me."

Marlie sighed. He was right. She didn't dare mention the blue feather, nor was she sure she ever would, but there was, indeed, a connection between them. Her grammie's Great Ones were probably tripping all over themselves, laughing.

On cue came the rumble of distant thunder.

Marlie rolled her eyes. The Great Ones could do with a little more imagination.

Well, she'd wanted someone to play with and here he was. "All right," she agreed heavily. "We'll be pals."

Caid looked at her.

"And roommates," she added. "But nothing more."

Another low rumble from the heavens sounded very much like a derisive chuckle.

"Guess what?" Marlie said, handing Caid his foam container of breakfast. She'd had her own breakfast at The Drugstore, but Caid didn't want to face an oblivious crowd again just yet, so she ordered his to go.

"I'm cured," Caid replied, digging into his scrambled eggs as if he hadn't eaten earlier with Waldo. Not that he'd eaten much, he told Marlie. Waldo dropped the plate of scrambled eggs when the coffeepot disappeared.

As a joke, it fell flat.

"Sorry," Marlie said gently. "You're still in a coma but are holding your own."

She paused. "What I wanted to tell you is there's a movie crew in town, looking for a site to film the latest Brad Pitt movie. Isn't that amazing?"

Caid shrugged. "Happens all the time. They come. They film. They go. The locals make a little extra money playing extras. The area hotels are full. There are star sightings in the restaurants, then things quiet down again. Happens every couple of years."

Which explained why only she and the rest of the

tourists were excited at the news, Marlie supposed. But still.

"This is *Brad Pitt,* we're talking about," she said.

"Who's he?"

"Oh, no one really." *Just the hunkiest of the current hunks.* "Jennifer Aniston's husband, is all."

"Ah," Caid replied knowingly.

Marlie shook her head, watching Caid spear a sausage. He hadn't a clue.

"Don't you ever watch television or go to the movies?"

"Sure I do. We have a dish at the ranch. CNN. This Week in History. And the next town over, Alpine, has a pretty good theater. I saw a Harry Potter movie there not long ago."

She blinked. *Harry Potter?*

"Yes, well. Word at The Drugstore this morning is this crew is looking for a more permanent location to give them a base. They plan to film other movies and commercials in the area and don't want to location hunt each time."

"Hmm," Caid replied absently. "Well, luck to 'em. So. What do you want to do today?"

"It may have escaped your notice," she answered, "but it's raining and Fort Davis seems an outdoors kind of town."

Caid grinned.

He had a devastating grin, Marlie thought. White straight teeth revealed themselves when his mouth curled up, and when the corners of his eyes crinkled, his sun-weathered skin contrasted with his green eyes and made them glow so that he seemed lit from within.

"I'm a rancher, Cutes. Rain never escapes my notice." He left his chair, tossed the breakfast container in the bedside trash receptacle, then strode to the window to look out in satisfaction.

"Won't last long," he pronounced. "But every bit helps. You don't melt, do you?"

"Not much. I brought your breakfast, and most of me is still here." She made a show of swiping at her damp shoulders. "Okay, what do you suggest we do? After all, you promised to play tour guide."

"I suggest we visit the fort. I haven't been there in years."

With old Fort Davis at the other end of town, they drove. The rain was really only a light mist and Marlie found that hers wasn't the only vehicle in the parking lot.

As they walked to the visitor's center, she gazed around curiously.

"No walls," she commented.

Caid grinned the grin that made her heart waggle.

"Tourist. No walls because it's a western Indian Wars military fort. It wasn't protecting itself, just providing a base and somewhere to live for the soldiers. The Apaches were some of the smartest and toughest fighters who ever lived, far too smart to attack a facility full of a couple of hundred soldiers. Any fighting was done away from the fort when the odds were more in the Indians favor."

"Uh-huh," Marlie replied.

But Caid was off and running. "In the west, walled forts were usually trading forts, not military installations," he told her, and a lot more besides. No wonder he preferred the History Channel.

They wandered through the enlisted men's barracks, restored to a company of buffalo soldiers who once called it home, according to the park employee dressed in period clothing who was there to tell them about it.

The man sent Marlie a strange look now and then when she replied—not to him but to the air next to her. Still, she did her best, passing on Caid's many questions for the docent as if they were her own.

It was all very interesting, but after awhile Marlie had had enough. Apparently Caid could talk military history all day.

"Thank you for your information," she told the docent at last, breaking into the man's discourse on period weapons, "but we need to go now. Uh, that is, *I* need to go now. There are other buildings to see."

She took Caid's hand and pulled, then dropped it like a hot potato when she caught the costumed soldier staring at her openmouthed.

"Um, bye." Marlie smiled weakly. "Thanks again." And she marched off, leaving Caid to follow. Or not.

"You could have just told me you were ready to go," Caid said, catching up to her.

"Sure I could. 'Let's go, Caid,' I could have said. Has a nice ring to it for a crazy woman."

"Well, why didn't you just nudge me or something?"

"I did. Twice. Your soldier buddy thinks I have a twitch."

Caid made a noncommittal noise in the back of his throat. "Why don't we go to the commanding officer's house? It's full of girl things."

It was, complete with Victorian furniture and a docent in a bustle. This time Marlie asked the questions while Caid wandered off to the back porch to stare up at the rocks forming a palisaded backdrop to the site.

It was a peaceful spot. He sat down on a step to enjoy the silence of the canyons beyond.

After a while, Marlie joined him. "Don't tell me you were bored?" she said teasingly.

"Nah. But when Mrs. Gallagher offered to show you how she tied her bustle, I figured it was time to get outta Dodge."

He liked her giggle. It bubbled forth like a fresh new spring in a parched pasture.

What could he do but laugh with her? A couple of days ago he'd thought he would never laugh again, but with this woman he laughed all the time.

"You know her?" Marlie asked.

"Mrs. Gallagher? She was my high school English teacher and my Sunday school teacher when I was about eight. I've been scared of her bustle all my life."

Marlie giggled again like he'd hoped she would, then glanced over her shoulder and sighed.

"Add Mrs. Gallagher to the list of those who think I'm certifiable," she said.

For lunch they went to the drive-through window of the burger place and took their meal to the roadside park just outside of town.

A huge cottonwood shaded the spot as it had for

half a century, and probably for that long the cement table under it had been a gathering place for locals—adults in the light of day; teenagers by the light of the moon.

Today, probably because of the rain earlier, they had the place to themselves.

Caid bit into his hamburger. "Good stuff," he said around a mouthful.

With better manners, Marlie swallowed before she laughed. "You're a bottomless pit, Caid. Do you always eat this much?"

"Only when I'm hungry. Usually I burn it off pretty fast, though. It's been years since I've been this sedentary."

"Oh? I think I feel a hike coming on. The state park has a trail I didn't have time for the other day. It's a short one. Only a mile and a half."

Caid gave a mock groan. "A mile and a half! Cutes, this is the Davis Mountains. That's a mile and a half of up, down, or sideways. Probably all three. I demand a nap first."

But before Marlie could reply, they heard a shrill appreciative wolf whistle. A car full of teenage boys had pulled up beside Marlie's SUV.

"Hey, darlin', wanna dance?" One of them deliberately raised the volume of the car radio sending an Alan Jackson tune bouncing off the rocks edging the small park.

Marlie merely looked bored and wagged a negative finger, but Caid stood abruptly.

"Why you little snot, Tim Chancelor. What the hell do you think you're doing making passes at respectable women?" he bellowed.

Tim, however, was unfazed. "C'mon, baby. We'll have us some fun, won't we guys?" He opened the car door.

"*Fun!* You little…"

Caid's soda cup hit the edge of the door, splattering coke and ice on the car, barely missing the boy just emerging from it.

The boy grinned. "You got a good aim, darlin'. Why don't you show us fellers how you did that?"

With a roar, Caid took a step forward, all set to tear the kid up when Marlie grabbed his arm.

"Let me handle this," she said. "Sorry about getting your car dirty," she called sweetly to the little horse's behind while Caid gritted his teeth.

Tim grinned wider.

"Tell your mom I'll be glad to have it washed. Oh, wait. Never mind. I'm supposed to see her for coffee later this afternoon. I'll tell her myself."

The boy stopped in his tracks. "Uh, you're going to my house?" he asked uncertainly.

"Why sure, honey. Your mom and I went to school together. We were best friends. I get back to Fort Davis to see her every chance I get. Don't you remember me? I used to change your diaper."

"Uh, no ma'am. I—I mean, yes ma'am. Guess we better be goin' now. Nice seeing you again."

"Nice seeing you, too, Timmy." She waved.

"What good manners that boy has," she said to Caid when the car took off at a much more sedate pace than when it arrived.

Caid laughed, watched Marlie calmly go back to nibbling her French fries, and laughed some more.

* * *

That night, Caid lay in bed, more relaxed than he'd been in months. The room was dark and he heard Marlie sigh softly as she, too, relaxed into sleep.

Friends, she'd made him promise. Well, he'd try.

Oh, he could stay out of her bed. For whatever reason, though he was hugely attracted to Marlie, especially after the kiss they'd shared at the ranch, sexuality wasn't an issue. It was there. He took a randy delight in that compact little body of hers.

But it wasn't an issue.

Being friends, however, was. Already his feelings for her were pushing the boundaries of friendship. He didn't think he'd ever enjoyed being with anyone more.

The woman had a gift for giving him back who he was, the man he'd all but forgotten he'd once been before the responsibilities of the ranch began to take their toll.

How long had it been since he'd taken time to get a fresh look at the land where he'd been born? He saw it so much he'd forgotten how beautiful it was, how steeped in history it was.

How long had it been since he'd had so much *fun?*

Turning over, Caid scrunched the pillow so that it fit better around his neck. What would they do tomorrow? he wondered sleepily.

Didn't matter. Closing his eyes, he felt his muscles relax into the comfort of the mattress.

Whatever it was, he was looking forward to it because no matter what they did afterward, his own day began with the intense pleasure of watching Marlie Simms wake up.

He sighed, and smiled and slept.

* * *

In room 305 of the Brewster County Memorial Hospital, Caid Matthews sighed, and smiled, and opened his eyes to gaze around the semidarkened room in confusion.

His head throbbed dully but when he lifted a hand to touch it, he found his arm attached to a needle, attached to a tube, attached to a hanging drip.

Using the other hand, he reached up and felt the rough edges of a bandage covering half his forehead. He also felt a couple of wires, but what they were a part of, he had no idea. Turning his head to find out made him nauseous.

A nurse entered the room, a broad smile plastered on her homely middle-aged face. "Hi, there, Mr. Matthews," she said cheerfully. "Nice to see you're awake. The doctor is on his way."

Well, hell.

Chapter Five

Marlie studied The Drugstore's breakfast menu. By now she had it almost memorized. Being just across the street from the hotel the restaurant's location was handy, but its busy, vocal clientele was what drew her back every morning. She loved listening to the gossip flowing around her and faithfully reported it back to Caid as soon as she returned to the room.

More than that, however, walking through the restaurant's doors made her feel immediately like part of the town. Locals and visitors to the area mingled freely here and no one sat shyly in a corner away from the hubbub.

Except herself.

Not that she was shy. All this generous exchange of information, however, meant that sooner or later a friendly someone would ask her about the person she took the carry-out breakfast to every morning.

And as soon as Marlie opened her mouth to prevaricate an answer, that someone would take one look at her telltale face and know she was lying through her teeth.

So she kept to herself, but watched and listened and enjoyed. And reported. After that traumatic first morning, Caid hadn't wanted to join her for close quarters in a public place again.

And Marlie was just as glad.

She sat by herself in The Drugstore every morning, in one of its back corners, and knew that everyone probably thought she was too snobby to mingle. Sitting in that same corner, talking to herself and giggling, however, would set up another train of thought all together.

Over the past few days, she and Caid had found too much in common to sit silently for long, though she supposed it could be done if they both bit their tongues.

Her downfall in public, however, would be their matching senses of humor. Out of all the people in the universe, she'd found a fellow punster. Who would have thought?

Marlie had loved puns for years, but learned at an early age that most of the world thought them the worst form of humor, so she kept what she found enormously funny to herself. Certainly she'd never shared her offbeat humor with Nicholas.

But Caid was a different story. His puns were just as delightfully awful as hers. They'd soon learned each other's signals. Whenever Caid's eyebrow twitched just so, she knew at once that he'd made a subtle pun and was watching to see if she'd caught it.

And whenever she laughed, the cowboy would grin broadly in satisfaction, and that would set Marlie off even more.

The really fun part, though, was that something in her face had the same effect on him.

"Ready to order, Ms. Simms?"

Linda placed a cup of coffee in front of her without Marlie having ordered it, a sure sign that the girl now considered Marlie a regular.

"A Spanish omelette, toast and orange juice this morning, Linda, and the usual to go."

"The usual" was enough breakfast to feed a lumber camp, but Caid wolfed it down with gusto.

Linda grinned. "That guy sure can..."

Around them, the low buzz of conversation rose a notch and a ripple of excitement spread through the room.

"Why, there's Caid Matthews!" Linda exclaimed.

And looking up, Marlie saw him, standing near the front door being greeted by a dozen people, some standing to shake hands and slap his back.

Caid. And everyone could see him.

For just a moment, Marlie knew sheer disappointment. He wasn't all hers anymore.

Then, jumping to her feet, she waved frantically, knowing that she, too, was grinning from ear to ear. Whatever it was that had been wrong was now right, and Caid was himself again.

At first he didn't see her as he joked and laughed with the people he knew.

"Caid," she called, not loudly, and she didn't think he heard her with the volume coming from the other tables. But he lifted his head to gaze in her direction, and their eyes met for a long silent moment.

Marlie felt her heart do a flip-flop and her wide smile waver with uncertainty. When she blinked, however, all was as it should be. Waving again, she pointed to the empty chair opposite her.

Caid nodded and began threading through the room toward her, stopping frequently at many of the tables in between to shake hands and exchange conversation here and there, telling those who asked that he was now right as rain, in spite of the bandage crowning one eye.

Finally, he sat down across from Marlie.

"Love the bandage, Uncle Caid," Linda said, giggling. "Makes you look mysterious."

"I'm gonna tell your daddy if you don't stop flirting with me, sweet cheeks," Caid replied, and winked at Marlie.

Linda giggled again. "You go right ahead, Uncle Caid. I've been flirting with you since I was a baby and you've been flirting back."

"In front of your daddy, maybe, but not in front of pretty ladies like this one here," and Caid nodded at Marlie. "And what will your boyfriend say?"

"Tim knows I love only him," Linda replied blithely. Then her expression changed. "Welcome home, Uncle Caid. We were worried about you," and she kissed Caid on the cheek.

Caid's smile for the teenager was enough to make Marlie's heart turn over again. "Thanks, Linda. It's good to be back," he said, his tone as gentle as his smile before he deliberately broke the moment.

"And I'm hungry. Hospital chow is only good if you're too sick to have any taste buds."

Linda laughed, as he'd obviously meant her to. "Coffee and lots of it, coming up. The usual?"

"Right on, darlin'."

When the girl left to turn in their order, Marlie gave a happy little bounce in her chair.

"Caid, I'm so happy for you. I know you've been anxious the last few days, but now things are back to normal. You probably want to get back to the Rolling M as quickly as you can."

Saying that last, and saying it cheerfully, ranked as one of Marlie's finest acting moments. Caid had needed her for a while, but he didn't anymore. He could now pick up his life where he'd left off, and a transient tourist would be nothing but a part of a stranger-than-fiction interlude.

"I reckon, darlin', you'd be right about that," he said.

Marlie had never heard his drawl quite so thick. Quite so...cynical. He'd never called her "darlin'" in that tone, either, and she wasn't sure she liked it.

But before she had a chance to comment, Linda appeared at their table, bringing Caid's coffee and refilling Marlie's.

"Your orders will be right out," she told them, and flitted off again.

Caid lifted his cup, but held it out invitingly.

Marlie smiled and lifted hers, too, and they clinked them together in a small toast.

"To breakfast," he said.

Breakfast. Toast. He didn't have to say it. Marlie

saw the pun written in the lift of Caid's eyebrow, and she laughed again.

When he grinned, too, her small niggle of uneasiness vanished.

"I'm going to miss you," she said.

The easy grin disappeared. "Are you now?" he drawled in that new way of his, and the uneasiness hopped right back into place.

"Well, in that case, darlin'…" he said, and this time the eyebrow hiked in a way Marlie didn't understand at all. "…maybe you just better tell me who you are."

Caid watched as the woman's face registered absolute shock.

Something wasn't right here. He knew it in his bones. When he'd seen her wave to him when he'd come in, he'd thought she looked familiar. Perhaps someone he'd met long ago, or danced with somewhere.

It hadn't mattered. She was merely an acquaintance, and for that reason alone he'd decided to sit with her rather than the many friends he had scattered throughout the room.

He just didn't feel like going through a blow-by-blow account—his mind acknowledged the pun—of the accident that landed him in the hospital.

But when he sat down at the table, he realized the woman was a complete stranger. She wasn't beautiful, but she was cute as a short-tailed pup, with a pair of the purest gray eyes he'd ever seen. He would have remembered those eyes.

Then she went all gushy over his recovery, and he

knew their purity was deceiving. He may have just taken a lump on the head, but he never forgot a woman. And this one, talking to him now as if she knew him very well, he'd never met before in his life. He was sure of it.

Another woman who wanted something, he thought cynically. But once bitten, twice cautious, as his dad used to say. Janice had walked off with all his ready cash, then fought him tooth and nail in the courts for half the ranch.

She didn't get it, but he'd never again allow a woman within snatching distance of anything he owned.

Somewhere in the hospital he'd lost his softer side, and he was keeping it that way.

Still, he'd give Cutes here points for catching and laughing at the toast pun.

Most people didn't care for puns and fewer still thought they were funny, but he'd always loved them. Because they could be thought annoying, he never shared the subtle word jokes, however.

But he'd known from the little wobble in the left corner of this cute little woman's luscious lips that they'd shared this one, even though it was one of the difficult silent kind that depended on a visual rather than a spoken word.

"You don't know who I am, Caid?" she asked him now, her gaze searching his face as if something important depended on his answer. He'd swear her gray eyes had a faint shimmer to them.

"Sorry," he said, almost feeling sorry for her. Almost.

She seemed to deflate a little. "Oh." And then she

drew a small breath. "I'm, um, Marlie. Marlie Simms. You must think me terribly rude."

Caid could be charming when he put his mind to it.

He put his mind to it.

"Not rude," he said. "Caring. And I appreciate it." He deliberately didn't comment on her earlier assumption of mutual friendliness.

"The whole town was talking about your accident," she said, as if that explained everything. He saw the uneasiness written all over her expressive face.

"Fort Davis is like that," he agreed. "You should see what happens when the Cub Scouts hold a pancake supper. We don't get much excitement, so every little thing becomes a major event."

"Except Brad Pitt," she replied.

"Pardon?"

"Um, did you know they're going to film a movie in this area?"

"Another one?" he asked without much interest.

But Linda was placing plates on the table, and Caid's stomach gave a soft, almost inaudible growl in anticipation. A big glass of milk, a small glass of orange juice, two eggs over easy, hash browns, grits, a biscuit with gravy, sausage, bacon and…toast.

For a microsecond, Caid found the wobble in the corner of the woman's mouth far more delectable than the food in front of him.

When she looked up and chuckled, he knew that without conscious thought his brow had twitched. It always did when something struck him as funny.

Now how had she known that?

For one of the few times in his life, Caid felt flustered. He didn't like it.

But Marlie Simms was already daintily eating her omelette, and Caid picked up his fork to dig into the feast in front of him.

Marlie swallowed her last bite of toast, not easy to do around the lump in her throat that had been steadily building throughout her breakfast. In the space since she'd left him shaving in the bathroom less than an hour ago, crossed the street and sat down at a table in The Drugstore, Caid had come back to himself.

And he didn't remember her at all.

It was as if someone she'd known all her life had given her a direct cut. Marlie felt bereft…and vaguely angry.

In the last few days of puttering around the Davis Mountains, seeing the sights, going to places Caid said he hadn't visited in years, they'd become…good friends.

Sure, Caid flirted with her. He was a cowboy, wasn't he? Cowboys began flirting when they put on their first pair of boots, and they took the art to their graves.

Didn't mean a thing. So what if it usually made Marlie's heart do a little skip? Big deal. She knew better than to take it seriously.

Lately, though, the tiny black dot on the blue feather Caid wore in his hatband had seemed to be winking at her.

Marlie paused, her coffee cup halfway to her lips. Was Caid wearing his hat when he came into the restaurant?

She didn't remember. But perhaps he'd hung it on one of the hat racks in the room before she'd seen him.

A quick scan, however, didn't reveal the Stetson with its distinguishing blue feather hanging on a peg anywhere.

She glanced at the cowboy opposite her, now wiping his mouth with his napkin.

He caught her gaze and held it for a moment, but it was a far different look than the one he'd sent her earlier. This look was calculating, suspicious.

Marlie shifted uneasily. She didn't know this man at all, she realized, and was quite certain he didn't want to know her. He would never believe that she'd spent the past few days playing around with his "ghost," for want of another word.

Nor was there time to explain had she wanted to. Caid stood, leaving a few bills for Linda's tip on the table.

"Thanks for allowing me to share your table, Ms. Marlie Simms," he said politely. "Hope you enjoy your visit to Fort Davis. You be careful now."

And he was gone, leaving Marlie no time to reply.

Slowly she took a sip of her fast-cooling coffee, feeling as if she'd just been slapped into reality.

In the face of the newly revitalized Caid Matthews' edgy masculinity, the past few days seemed as weird an episode as any a Hollywood film could produce.

Had she dreamed it then? Was her mind playing tricks with her? Perhaps she should check out ginkgo biloba.

When Linda never brought her the bill, Marlie

walked to the register, and found that Caid had paid it.

Of course.

But Linda held out a bag with a large foam container in it. Caid's breakfast, Marlie realized. The one she'd ordered for him before he'd joined her.

"I didn't tell Uncle Caid about this one," Linda said, grinning at her. "I figured what he doesn't know won't hurt him, if you know what I mean."

Marlie summoned a smile. "Thanks. I appreciate it."

She dug in her wallet and paid the girl with the money Caid had insisted on giving her earlier in the hotel room. They had the same argument every morning.

But never again, Marlie thought.

"You know, this is the same breakfast Uncle Caid ordered," Linda chattily. "Isn't that weird?"

"Weird," Marlie agreed.

When she neared the steps of the hotel, Marlie saw Waldo's ancient pickup toward the end of the line of cars parked in front. Waldo sat on the driver's side.

He waved but didn't speak, and she waved back but didn't stop.

She wasn't surprised, then, when she found Caid in the hotel's lobby talking to Ann, a duffel bag at his feet.

When Marlie would have passed by them, however, Ann stopped her.

"Marlie, this is Caid Matthews. He's the one who booked your room and then was in the accident."

"We've met," Caid told the desk clerk easily, and turned to Marlie with a smile.

"I'm sorry. I didn't realize we had a hotel room in common when we had breakfast this morning."

She politely smiled back. Over the past few days, she'd found Caid's smile devastating, but this one just didn't seem to have the same wattage as the others.

"Caid believes he left his hat in the room," Ann said. "Did you see it?"

Marlie blinked. "His hat?"

"It has a snakeskin hatband, with a blue feather stuck in it."

For a moment, Marlie thought he looked a little self-conscious.

"Brings me luck," he added, the tips of his ears going an interesting pink.

Ann laughed. "Ha! You weren't so lucky when you hit that pine tree."

"Wasn't wearing my hat," Caid replied simply.

The banter sounded just like the Caid Marlie knew, and then it struck her.

Caid hadn't been wearing his hat when he came to breakfast, she thought. *This Caid didn't have his hat!*

"I, um…I'll see if I can find it," she said, and practically raced up the stairs.

Sure enough, when she threw open the door to the room she found Caid, fully dressed except for his boots, lying on his bed reading one of her romance novels.

"What I'd like to know," he drawled, without looking up, "is why a rancher who uses spurs on a perfectly good horse gets the beautiful girl in the end.

Any man who uses spurs on a horse ought be run out of the West.''

"You're here!" Marlie exclaimed.

Then he did look at her. "Uh-huh.''

"Your hat is here.''

"Yes, it is. Right there on the dresser. Why?''

"There's a man downstairs who wants it.''

Caid's eyes narrowed to slits, and his posture slowly changed from loose and lazy to broad-shouldered and intimidating.

"Who?''

"You,'' Marlie said baldly.

"Come again?''

"You're here, Caid,'' Marlie exclaimed. "Downstairs. You're out of the hospital. People can see you. Hear you. And I had *breakfast* with you!'' she wailed, and burst into tears.

Again.

Twice this week, first with Waldo, now with Caid.

Enough already, she thought blearily, but couldn't make the tears stop.

Caid was off the bed in a heartbeat and had her wrapped in his strong capable arms. "No, you didn't, Cutes. My breakfast is right here in the bag in your hand. I can smell it.''

Marlie lifted her head to stare up at him. "But I did, Caid. And you ate the exact same things I ordered for you. Now you're downstairs in the lobby talking to Ann. And...and you want your hat.''

She felt Caid stiffen.

"I don't know who the hell is downstairs,'' he said gruffly, "but nobody's taking my hat.''

"But...''

"I mean it, Marlie. You tell whoever it is that's come calling that his hat isn't here because this one's *mine*," and he strode to the dresser and plopped the hat under discussion onto his head.

While he was at it, he grabbed up a couple of tissues and returned to Marlie to gently mop her face.

"Hush now, Cutes," he said softly. "The hat's my concern, not yours. You don't need to worry at all," and he brushed her cheek with his lips.

At least, that was how it started out. His lips met her cheek, and paused. Stopped.

Marlie stood absolutely still, every sensory nerve in her face mesmerized by the feel of Caid's lips against her skin. For long moments his lips stayed there, and she knew...*knew*...that everything in him wanted to home in on her mouth instead, because everything in her wanted it, too.

But at last she felt the soft exhalation of breath against her cheek—a sigh, she thought, to match her own—and then his lips were gone, replaced by his smooth-shaven cheek.

"Well, hell," he said, and stepped away.

Caid knew as soon as he saw Marlie Simms slowly descending the hotel staircase—without his hat—that she'd been crying.

He might barely know the woman, might find her suspicious as all get out, but it was all he could do not to take the stairs three at a time, find the horse's rear who'd made her cry and punch him out.

"I'm sorry," she said when she came up to him. "I didn't...uh, it wasn't... It's not there," she said in a rush.

Well, hell, Caid thought. The woman was lying through her teeth. Now what?

But he damn sure wasn't leaving without his hat.

"You're sure?" he asked, just to give her some rope. Or a second chance, whichever she preferred.

"Y-yes, I'm sure."

Liar. What was there about him that made women he could like do nothing but lie to him? "You looked?"

"Oh, yes. I looked," she replied brightly.

An honest answer, Caid thought cynically. She *had* looked. But she wasn't telling what she saw.

He smiled. "Then you won't mind if I look, too, will you?"

Chapter Six

Caid's long, lanky stride had him halfway up the staircase before Marlie recovered enough to hightail it after him.

Oh, my goodness. Oh, my goodness! "Wait," she commanded breathlessly.

He halted. "Yes?"

Never had she heard so much danger in one little word.

"It's locked."

The man just stood there as if he'd kick the door down if he had to, but Marlie had had enough.

Head high and back straight, she passed him on the stairs, putting a deliberate and defiant sashay into her hips as she led him the rest of the way up the old-fashioned steps.

At the door of the room, she rattled the key in the lock as loudly as she could before opening it. Then, stepping back, she allowed Caid to pass in front of her.

Whatever happened now would just have to happen, she supposed.

Caid stood near the window, wearing his boots and hat and ready for anything, when Marlie and the stranger came through the door with a rattle of keys and locks.

The fellow looked familiar, but Caid was sure he didn't know him. Whoever he was, though, he was a low-down son of a gun if he thought he could just waltz in and steal a man's hat. The weasel would have to take it off his head first, and that wasn't going to happen.

It was a moot point, however, when the man's snake-eyed gaze slowly traveled around the room, passing over Caid without a flicker.

Ha! Another one who couldn't see him or hear him.

Grinning at Marlie, Caid caught her eye and winked.

But she just stood there looking sad. "Oh, Caid," she said softly.

He frowned. "What?"

She shook her head.

"Dammit, Cutes…"

"I don't see it, Ms. Simms. Do you mind if I check the bathroom?"

"Don't let him, Marlie."

"Go ahead," she said.

As the man headed for the bathroom, Caid went to stand beside Marlie. "Cutes," he said earnestly, "this guy's way out of bounds. You don't have to take this…."

But the snake's underbelly was back, looking none

too pleased. "You're sure you don't have a souvenir of your stay tucked away somewhere?" he asked.

With a curse, Caid started toward him only to have Marlie grab his arm. "Let him look," she said. "It's the only way he'll be satisfied."

The slime gave Marlie an odd look, but she ignored it, instead going to her suitcase and opening it to show him it was empty. Then she opened dresser drawers to show him they were full.

When he stared a little too long for Caid's liking at the frothy undergarments displayed there, Marlie pursed her mouth and shook her head warningly and Caid subsided.

He gave the man an earful, though, then wondered if the worm, looking a little red around the gills, might've picked up on some of it.

Marlie suggested he look in the wardrobe, too, but the man finally had sense enough to shake his head.

"My mistake," he said, and slunk out the door.

Oh, the fellow's back was straight, his shoulders squared and his head high, but he *slunk* nevertheless. Caid knew it, and knew the polecat knew it, too.

"You idiot!" he called loudly, just as the man pulled the door shut behind himself.

The door seemed to pause a moment, then gently closed.

"Oh, Caid, I'm so sorry," Marlie said sadly.

He looked at her in confusion. "What?"

Caid closed the door softly behind him, feeling like all the names he'd called himself in there. Marlie Simms didn't have his hat, and he'd known it almost as soon as he walked into the room.

What the hell was he thinking, to go through her things that way?

But if she didn't have his hat, who did? The roommate no one had seen fit to mention? The one whose half-eaten breakfast sat on the bedside table? The one who occupied the other obviously slept-in bed?

Man or woman? he wondered.

At the thought of it being a man, Caid felt an unfamiliar spurt of heat churn through his gullet. Still, if it was a man, only one of the beds would have been used.

"Didn't find it?" Ann asked as he strode through the lobby.

"Nah. Who's her roommate?"

Ann laughed. "Now that's a great mystery. Housekeeping makes up two beds and cleans up after two people. There's a man's clothing hanging in the wardrobe. But no one ever sees him."

She shrugged. "As you can imagine, curiosity is eating us all alive. But we rent by the room, not by the number of people in it, so no one wants to ask. I take that back. We *want* to, but no one will. Marlie checked in by herself."

The wardrobe, Caid thought. The one place he'd finally been too embarrassed to look. But if the mysterious roommate did have his hat, the creampuff was probably wearing it.

"Funny thing," Ann continued. "When she first arrived, Marlie came downstairs one evening saying she heard an intruder in her room. I checked, but no one was there, and she never mentioned it again."

"Guess he took up residence," Caid said lightly,

and headed out the door. Waldo was probably fit to be tied at being kept waiting.

One thing for sure, though. Marlie Simms hadn't seen the last of Caid Matthews. He wanted his hat.

More importantly, he wanted his lucky jay feather.

"Caid," Marlie said. "We have to talk."

Caid eyed the congealed eggs in his half-eaten breakfast with distaste.

"What about?" he asked, taking a bite of cold bacon.

"You."

He wrapped a link of sausage in a slice of cold toast spread with grape jelly. "What about me?"

Marlie watched in frustration as Caid salvaged what he could of his breakfast, seemingly not the least concerned over what had just occurred.

"You just walked through the door and didn't see yourself," she replied dryly. "*And* you saw yourself walk through the door and didn't recognize yourself. You don't find that a tad unusual?"

"No, because the lowlife who was here isn't me. I'm handsomer, for one thing." He grinned.

She was not amused. "It *was* you," she said. "And why do you call yourself a lowlife?"

"Because only a stink bug goes through a woman's things looking for a stupid hat when she said she didn't have it," Caid replied roughly. "Marlie, couldn't you *see* what that guy is? He's a rat's behind, a petty money-grubbing Scrooge. I'm not like that."

But he rubbed a hand over the back of his neck. "God, I hope I'm not like that. *Am* I like that?"

"No," Marlie replied instantly. "And I'd bet your

ranch on it.'' Walking over, she gave him a one-armed hug.

She knew better than to use two.

"But we still need to talk,'' she added. "You can show me where you wrecked your truck.''

The once majestic ponderosa pine lay at the side of the road, its base a jagged splinter. On the road itself, black tread marks showed where Caid had stomped on the brakes and swerved to miss the deer on that early evening over a week ago.

He was lucky to be alive, Marlie thought.

And Caid *was* alive. The man standing beside her, silently examining the tree that had totaled his truck and almost totaled him, most definitely wasn't a ghost.

But if not, what was he?

It was a question they both needed answered. Caid, because he needed the answer to come to grips with himself. And Marlie…well, just because.

The other Caid needed it answered, too, but at the moment, after his brush with death, his boots were probably too firmly planted on the ground to be able to deal with something he couldn't see or hear.

Besides, as magnetic as the other one was, it was this Caid who mattered most to her, Marlie thought.

Just off the side of the road was a stand of trees with a large flat boulder in their midst. Climbing onto it, they opened the bag of chips she'd bought before they left town and popped the tops on a couple of cans of soda.

"How do you keep your boyish figure?'' she asked

Caid with a laugh as he dug a chip into a carton of avocado dip.

"Work it all off," he said. "Usually, anyway. Things are quiet right now, but I'll have to get back to the Rolling M pretty soon. Waldo can't handle it alone for long."

Marlie didn't tell him that he was probably already back at the ranch, even as they spoke. Some part of him had to know that.

She took a swig of soda and listened to the bird chatter in the trees around them. It reminded her of her blue feather. For whatever reason, she'd taken to carrying it around with her, keeping it tucked in her shirt pocket where it was hidden or the top of it barely showing.

Caid, always wearing its partner in his hat, had never noticed.

She wasn't sure what Gram's Great Ones had in mind with this farce, but she knew Caid needed far more than a blue feather to get him out of the mess he was in, whether he believed he was in a mess or not.

She didn't have a Master's degree in psychology and counseling for nothing.

"Do you mind if I pose a few questions?" she asked him quietly.

"I don't have anything to hide. Fire away."

"I'm going to get personal," she warned.

"I like it when you're personal, Cutes." Caid waggled his eyebrows.

Marlie laughed. "I'm serious."

"So am I. Get personal."

"When you had the accident, why were you coming into town to spend the night?"

"Ah, *that* kind of personal. I had an appointment first thing in the morning with the bank, and afterwards, I was going to see a Realtor. By staying at the Limpia, I didn't have to drive into town so early."

"But you went back to the ranch."

He shrugged. "I'd forgotten the papers I needed."

"Papers?"

"Titles. I meant to sell five hundred acres, and was borrowing money against the sale."

"Ouch," Marlie said.

"Damn right, ouch. And it wasn't necessary, dammit. There has to be some way to pay the bills without selling off the ranch a piece at a time. The Matthews have held their land for three generations. Why does it have to be the fourth one to carve it up? I would never sell my land. Not in a million years."

"But you were doing it."

"No, I wasn't. I...well, yes, but I didn't want to. It's just plain *wrong!* And so is putting Waldo out to pasture. He's been a cowhand all his life. It's all he knows."

Both of them ignored the pun.

"Waldo?"

Caid sighed. "The ranch can't afford his salary anymore," he explained tiredly. "My dad set him up with a healthy pension plan, but Waldo has to retire to get it. Everybody knows the old goat would take to retirement the way this morning's buzzard's belly would take to food poisoning. If it didn't kill him, he'd wish it had."

Hurling a stick at an innocent pine seedling, Caid

growled, "But did that cut any ice? Hell, no. He was all set to tell Waldo he had to retire."

Marlie stilled. "He?"

"Me, I guess. I. But I wouldn't have done it. Hell, I *couldn't* have done it. Waldo's been a second father to me and was a good friend to my dad when he was alive."

There's a pattern here, Marlie thought.

"So you were returning to town after picking up the forgotten papers."

"Yeah." Caid grinned suddenly. "And arguing with myself, just like I'm doing now. Sorry, Cutes."

"Were you arguing with yourself when you hit the tree?"

"I don't know. I'm not sure I remember. But probably. Why?"

"Because you seem to have been of two minds when the accident occurred," Marlie said slowly. "Maybe you just didn't have time to pull yourself together, and one self went one way and the other self went to…to the hospital."

Caid chuckled. "Maybe."

He fished around for the remaining tortilla chip and swiped it around the near empty dip container. "But I doubt it."

Waldo drove like a comatose turtle. Before leaving Fort Davis, they'd stopped at the grocery store and then for gas. By now, Caid was tired and his head was beginning to throb.

He wished he had his hat. He'd use it to cover his eyes and take a little nap. As it was, they hurtled up the road like a chase scene in slow motion and he watched the scenery leisurely roll by.

At this rate, they'd be home sometime next week.

"Comin' up around the next curve is where you hit that tree," Waldo said, speaking for the first time in over an hour.

Caid sat up. He didn't remember much about the accident except the deer jumping in front of him. He knew, though, that he was lucky to be alive. What a fool he'd been not to wear his seat belt. Still, he'd lost that fool for good, he hoped.

When at last they rounded the curve, Waldo used his chin to point at the fallen tree. A late model SUV was parked by the side of the road near it.

With ample time to examine the spot, Caid's heart slowed to the speed of Waldo's driving as mortality tapped him on the shoulder. How easily the Matthews' ranch could have become a ward of the state.

After his divorce, he'd changed his will, leaving the ranch to a state land preservation society. But only because there had been no one else to leave it to. If he'd died a week ago, his branch of the Matthews' family would have died with him.

Better get used to it, though, he thought. He damn sure didn't plan to marry again. Not even for the sake of the Matthews' name would he forfeit his land to another scheming woman.

From a fiancée who got cold feet two weeks before their wedding only to marry someone else a month later, to Janice who'd been after his ranch from the get-go, to Marlie Simms who would stoop to hiding a man's hat, Caid had had all the lying women he could stand.

The idea of never having kids, though, made him feel a little sick.

A flicker of blue caught his eye, and he saw a figure back in the trees. Branches obscured a clear view, however.

The owner of the SUV, he imagined. Probably a geology student from the nearby university.

Again a flash of blue captured his attention, and Caid saw a jay flitting among the branches of the tree that had damned near killed him, its needles already turning brown on broken limbs thrust upward and outward in odd angles.

The sight made him think of his hat.

Just you wait, Marlie Simms. Just you wait.

As Caid finished off the chips, Marlie let her gaze drift around the pleasant spot. The branches of the trees surrounding them sighed and whispered in the light breeze, their shadow patterns shifting in counterpoint on the ground, a wide blue sky above it all.

A peaceful scene, but one she barely acknowledged.

I'm not involved. Okay, she'd asked a few questions. What of it? Caid could handle this however he wanted.

Hadn't she refrained from pointing out that against all natural laws, he'd become a split personality in the most literal sense? Hadn't she kept silent the fact that the only way he was going to pull himself together— again, literally—was to confront himself?

This was Caid's problem and she was most definitely through giving advice. She'd already played God once and it darn near cost her her job.

For sure it had cost a fiancé.

Most importantly, however, it had put a teenage girl in physical danger and landed the child on the streets.

Seeing to it the girl was rescued was no excuse for Marlie's own lack of judgment. Because of her stupid Pollyanna advice, the fifteen-year-old had wound up in the hospital. The child had been lucky not to lose the baby she was carrying.

Marlie sighed.

"What's the matter, Cutes?"

"Nothing."

"You listened to me. Now I want to listen to you," Caid said, giving her his complete attention. "Spit it out."

"I was only thinking about my job," Marlie replied, hoping he'd leave it alone.

"No, you weren't."

She blinked. "Was too."

"A job makes you laugh," Caid said seriously. "It makes you frustrated or it makes you mad. But it doesn't make you sigh. So let's have it."

And for the first time, aside from skimming the high points to her grandmother, Marlie gave it to him.

"I'm an assistant counselor at a high school in San Antonio," she began slowly. "And right before school was out we had an…incident."

Could she really tell this to Caid?

Yes, she thought. Very possibly she could tell this man anything.

"It involved a fifteen-year-old girl, Marcia, who came to me because she was pregnant. Deliberately, she said, because she wanted a baby. Someone to love her no matter what. Those were her words. She planned to marry her boyfriend and they would live happily ever after in their own little house with their own little family.''

Caid put a comforting arm around her shoulders.

''But when it was too late, Marcia found out the boyfriend's plans didn't include babies or becoming a husband. So I advised her to tell her parents.''

Caid handed her a napkin.

''Marcia tried to tell me,'' she said gruffly, ''but I just didn't get it. I talked her into telling her mother, who told her father.''

He kissed her hair.

''Her father beat her up and threw her out of the house. She called me and I took her to the hospital. When she got out the next morning, I took her home with me. This was on a weekend.''

Using the napkin, Marlie blew her nose.

''I arrived at school on Monday, and her father was there. He told the principal I'd aided and abetted a runaway.''

''Did the principal stand up for you?''

''In a manner of speaking. I'd acted irresponsibly and should have realized that taking students into my home was unprofessional, he said. As a professional, I should have notified the proper juvenile authorities, filled out the proper paperwork, etcetera, but left the girl strictly alone.''

Marlie laughed bitterly. ''Then he fell all over himself appeasing the father so the school wouldn't be sued. With the father being appeased, the principal offered me another chance. It's hard to find school

counselors these days. However, he warned my immediate supervisor to keep an eye on me.''

"And?''

"My immediate supervisor was my fiancé. He
didn't like keeping an eye on someone in disgrace
who wore his ring on her finger, so he asked for it
back.''

"Stupid bastard,'' Caid said. "You're lucky to be
rid of him.''

"I think so, too. But, still, I'm never ever giving
advice again,'' she replied. "Because of me, that
child was beat up. Because of me, she could have lost
her baby, and because of me, she did lose her parents.
She's now living in a group house.''

From his position beside her on the boulder, Caid
cradled her in one of his big comforting hugs.

"You really know how to beat up on yourself,
don't you, Cutes? You have to know there was nothing else you could have done.''

"I could have left well enough alone.''

"No, you couldn't. It's impossible for you to allow
someone to hurt without you trying to help them.
Hands on, not shuffling papers. That's just who you
are, Marlie Simms.''

"Not anymore. I'm never giving anyone advice
again.''

Caid laughed. "Not even to me?'' he asked, with
mocking self-pity. "Here I am, a noperson to everyone in the world but you, and you're just going to
leave me hanging?''

"Especially not to you,'' she said.

Again, his laughter rumbled under her ear. "Ah,
Cutes, you can give me advice anytime.''

But Marlie lifted her head sharply, banging it against his chin.

"Sorry," she murmured.

Through the overhanging branches she watched a battered old pickup slowly pass by her parked SUV. It seemed to pause a moment, but kept on going until the intervening trees hid it from view.

Waldo, she thought, taking Caid home. She'd thought he was already there.

A blue jay flew up from the withering branches of the felled pine tree, crying raucously.

Shut up, Marlie told it silently, and placed her head on Caid's accommodating shoulder, more than willing to shut out the world for a while with someone who'd already done it.

Chapter Seven

Caid let himself out the barn door and automatically reached up to pull his hat a little farther down on his brow. The brim had an unfamiliar feel to it, mainly because it was the old straw one he'd used two summers ago.

Dammit, he wanted his good hat back. Aside from the fact it was new—well, almost new; he'd bought it for his court appearance last year—it had his jay feather.

And wasn't that a hell of a thing, him missing that old feather like he did?

Since he'd stuck it in his hat at fifteen, he'd been teased about wearing it over the years. Had even poked fun at himself over it. Lately, he'd felt it was a sort of worn-out signature, that the feather no longer meant anything to him but a habit outgrown long ago but still retained.

Now, however, he couldn't seem to get the damn

thing out of his mind. When he'd wakened in the hospital, the first thing he'd asked for was his hat, then remembered leaving it at the hotel when he'd returned to the ranch for the papers he'd forgotten.

When the Simms woman told him it wasn't in the room, he'd been miffed at her needless lying but not overly concerned. Yet once back at the ranch, the loss of the blamed thing had begun to haunt him.

He might never confess it to a living soul, but dammit, he just didn't feel right without his good luck feather.

Incomplete. That was the word.

Waldo was at the stove scrambling eggs when he entered the kitchen.

"You say you met Marlie Simms?" Caid asked by way of greeting, hanging his featherless hat on the peg by the door.

"Yeah, I met her."

"What did you think of her?"

"Nice girl. Can't lie worth a durn, though."

Caid sent the old man a sharp look. Now what brought that on? he wondered.

"You noticed it, too, then," he replied dryly. "So, she lied to you?"

"Thought about it. Changed her mind."

"And what was she thinking of lying about?"

"You," Waldo replied laconically. "But she didn't."

After years with the old man, Caid knew the signs. "You're not going to give me the details, are you?"

"Nope. No harm done. Like I said, she's a nice girl. Carries a jay feather in her pocket."

"*What?*"

"You heard me," Waldo said.

"She told me she didn't have my hat."

"I didn't say she did. I said she has a feather."

"Yeah," Caid said bitterly. "My feather."

"Didn't say that, either."

Caid grabbed the straw hat off the peg. "I'm going into town."

"Don't you want some breakfast?"

"I'll eat at The Drugstore."

Sure enough, as soon as he walked through the double screen doors of The Drugstore, Caid spied Marlie Simms sitting at the same back table where she'd been last time.

She didn't see him, though, but sat with her cheek resting against one fist as she studied the menu.

For a brief moment, he thought she looked kind of sad, but then he got himself in hand. The woman had his feather.

"Same list there as yesterday," he said easily, sitting down across from her uninvited.

She looked up, startled, before her gaze turned wary. "Good morning," she said.

"Mind if I sit down?"

She smiled, a sweet smile to go with her guileless, lying gray eyes.

"Yes," she replied, then widened the smile to a grin. "Just kidding. But you take a lot for granted."

"Only empty chair in the house."

Making a show of it, she looked around the room full of half-filled tables, and lifted an eyebrow.

Caid studied the menu.

"Seat yourself," she replied, deadpan.

Before he could stop it, his eyebrow jerked, but when he looked up, Marlie, too, was studying the menu as if it held detailed directions for world peace.

The corner of her mouth quirked the least bit, he noticed.

He noticed too, that when Linda came with their coffee and took their order, Marlie made a point of telling the girl it would be separate checks.

Then, flicking a quick glance at Caid, she added, "And the usual to go, please."

A clear challenge.

"Sure thing, Ms. Simms."

Caid magnanimously allowed Marlie time enough for three or four sips of coffee. Even he wouldn't attack a woman before she'd had her morning caffeine.

"Nice feather," he said, looking pointedly at the breast pocket of her touristy summer-vacation golf shirt where the top edge of a blue feather barely showed.

After her choking fit and keeping his tone bland, he added, "I used to have one just like it."

"It's not yours," she said flatly, and glared at him.

"No?"

"No."

Had she left it alone they would probably have been at an impasse because, for some reason, Caid was finding himself not quite able to come right out and accuse the woman. Those darn gray eyes of hers, he supposed.

Fortunately for him, she felt she had to explain. "I found it in San Antonio just as I was leaving to come out here."

"Lots of blue jays in central Texas, is there?"

"Well, no. They're not common in the city at all. That…that's why I kept it. It's lucky."

"For the right owner." Caid did his best to make his tone sound menacing. "There's an old Native American legend that says. if you steal a blue jay's feather, Brother Coyote will eat you up."

Marlie, apparently, wasn't menaced. She laughed.

"My grammie is part Indian and that's not what she says. Besides, I didn't steal this one."

Caid tried again. "And what does Grammie say?"

"She says… You don't want to know what she says."

"But I do," Caid said softly.

When she looked undecided for a moment, he knew immediately that the woman didn't like what she was getting ready to say, so it would probably be a lie.

"She said that when I find my feather's match, I'll have found my… That is, I'll have found a very good friend."

"Grammie needs to double-check her Indian lore," Caid replied coldly. "No two fingerprints, or feathers, match exactly."

He didn't know if that was true or not, but it didn't matter. This cute little city woman needed to realize that in West Texas, hat stealers were lower than dirt and he wasn't about to let her get away with it, let alone be her "very good friend."

But in spite of his best scowl, Marlie didn't look threatened at all.

"That's what I told her," she replied.

And she wore her sad look again, the one that could tug at his heart strings…if he still had one.

Which he didn't. His accident might have totaled his truck, but it had also totaled the part of himself that was a pushover. He wasn't quite sure how it had happened, but he was liking it just fine.

Linda brought their breakfasts, and as they each silently dug into the food before them, Caid took the opportunity to plan strategy.

It was time, he decided, to change tactics. He'd bring out the big guns.

Hadn't his mother always claimed her boy could charm the honey from the bees?

Besides, there was something delightfully appealing about charming Marlie Simms. Not only would it serve the cute little feather thief right, the feather in her breast pocket would be his again in no time.

He ate the last bite of sausage, placed his knife and fork across his plate and wiped his mouth with his napkin.

Capturing the woman's suddenly wary silver gaze, he smiled.

Marlie's heart plummeted.

Caid Matthews' smile was a slow devastation of sensuous lips bracketed by long thin dimples on either side. And he'd aimed it directly at her.

Every sense of self-preservation sounded immediate alarm.

Hearts had been broken over that smile, she'd bet, but hers darn sure wasn't going to be one of them.

It was bad enough that the Caid upstairs at the hotel could melt her heart at the drop of a gentle tease. This one in the flesh caused her own flesh to sensitize to the point of sunburn.

Caid in spirit might still be one hundred percent male, but his very human self spilled it right over the top.

Run, she shouted silently to her jelly-kneed legs. But her traitorous feet kept her seated, as mesmerized as a bird enthralled by a cobra.

"You've been to the fort," Caid was saying. "But how would you like to…"

Suspicion thankfully snapped her out of enchantment. "How do you know I've been to the fort?"

Caid's face went totally blank. "Well, uh, just guessed, I suppose. You've been here a few days and most tourists take in the old fort if they haven't seen it before. It's an interesting place."

"Yes, I know. I've been there," she replied, grudgingly, to his questioning look.

He managed to hide most of his triumph, she noticed.

"Well, how would you like to see a *mystery,*" he asked, dropping his voice to give the word added drama, "that may or may not be related to the old fort? I'll show you something most tourists never even notice."

Marlie was immediately intrigued, but she also knew danger when it smiled at her.

"Sorry," she said. "I have other plans." She would ask the Caid she could manage—more or less—what *mystery* this one was talking about.

"You have to go on private property," the man across from her replied, just as if he'd read her mind. "Your friend won't be able to take you there."

"What friend?"

"Your roommate. The one you take breakfast to every morning."

Oh, lordy. Should she tell this man that it was *he* who was her "roommate?" "Um, he's not exactly a…a friend…."

Caid's eyebrow lifted. "He?"

Marlie colored. "Not that kind of he. He's a friend. I mean, he's not a friend, but he…you…he—he's just a…roommate. Sort of."

"Sort of," he echoed, his tone full of insinuation.

But Marlie had had enough. Even to those most involved, the situation was unexplainable, and she was through trying to explain it.

It was none of her business, after all. In a few days she would be going back to San Antonio. The one Caid could room with whoever had the hotel room after her. Or not.

The other Caid could take his sexy green eyes and come-hither smile and hit on the next tourist to cross his path. Or not.

If the stubborn man—men—couldn't get it together, too bad. She was outta here.

She stood. "Thanks for the invitation, but I'm sure you have a lot of business to take care of this morning now that you're out of the hospital. The…the bank or real estate office or something."

Pulling out a couple of bills for her share of the tip, she smiled down at the cowboy, still seated and frowning up at her.

"Good luck with your ranch," she added politely. "I hope things work out all right for it. And with Waldo."

Tomorrow, she vowed, hurrying through the restaurant's double doors, she was having breakfast somewhere else.

That is, if she was here tomorrow. She just might return to San Antonio earlier than originally planned. After all, she'd come to Fort Davis to get away from it all and landed right in another predicament.

She sighed. If she'd been smart a few moments ago, she would have just given Caid the feather in her pocket and been done with it. After all, the feather is what he really wanted. The hat was just an excuse.

But when had she ever been smart? Besides, she wanted to keep her blue feather. It was a…a souvenir.

"I had breakfast with you again this morning," she told Caid as soon as she walked into the room.

He was just coming out of the bathroom, bare chested, and making swipes at his still dripping hair with the ends of a towel slung round his neck…and looking good enough to eat.

It was definitely time she went home.

"Couldn't have, Cutes. I'm starving."

Marlie wasn't in the mood. "No, you're not," she replied tartly. "You just ate enough to put a sumo wrestler to shame."

He lifted an eyebrow. "What brought this on?"

"You, Caid," she burst out with sudden frustration. "Both of you. You've got to *do* something."

"Well, hell, Marlie. I am doing something," Caid replied hotly. "I'm having breakfast. And for your information, I was taking a shower while you were across the street making goo-goo eyes at some yo-yo who'd sell his own mother for a buck."

He plopped the foam container from The Drugstore on the nightstand, opened it, and sat down on the side of the bed. But instead of digging into sausage, bacon, hash browns, grits, a couple of eggs, biscuit and gravy, he scowled at them.

"What do you expect me to do, Marlie?" he asked tiredly, not looking at her.

"Confront yourself, Caid. You can't ignore yourself forever, you know."

He huffed an ironic laugh. "What you call ignoring, I call avoiding a complete stranger. That bozo isn't me, Cutes. How many times do I have to tell you?"

But Marlie was busy switching her sandals for her hiking boots.

"That bozo thinks I stole his hat," she said. "The one, and I'm quoting here, with his lucky blue feather. I suggest you give it back to him, or he might just decide to take it from you."

Caid picked up his fork. "Let him try. Besides, my jay feather is lucky for no one but me."

"For the life of me, I can't see that you've been so darn lucky lately," Marlie replied, gathering her hat and water bottle.

"I'm out of here today, Caid," she continued. "By myself. There's a hiking trail I'd like to try and I think I need to go it alone this time."

He nodded. "But be careful, Cutes. This is rugged country. It's easy to turn an ankle. And watch for snakes. Matter of fact, why don't you take my hat?"

Leaving his breakfast, he fetched the hat in question, took hers off and plopped his hat on her head.

"Looks good on you," he said, pushing it back off

her nose. "My lucky feather probably works for you, too, you know."

And he brushed her cheek with his lips.

Marlie closed her eyes, wanting to throw her arms around this sweet dear man, so willing to share what the other Caid wanted back so badly. She also wanted to kick his gorgeous tush.

Sighing, she took the hat off her head and gave it back to the man half-embracing her.

"Thanks," she said, stepping back. "But I already have one," and she showed him the one in her pocket. After all, he'd seen it now.

Caid gazed at her feather in astonishment.

"Why, it looks just like mine," he exclaimed, taking the feather from his hat and holding it next to hers in comparison. "Where did you get it?"

"I found it in San Antonio, just before I left."

The effect of her words was instantaneous. Caid stilled, and suddenly Marlie found her gaze locked with his as his green eyes darkened to deepest jade.

"Cutes," he said softly, "I think we're a pair," and he reached for her.

"No!"

Scared silly that she would walk into the man's mesmerizing embrace, scared silly that her stupid heart was taking her in a direction she didn't want to go, Marlie backed up a good three feet.

"It's just coincidence," she said breathlessly. "And—and the fact that I can see you. That's all."

But Caid shook his head, his gaze never leaving her face, though he made no move to follow her panicked retreat.

"That's not all, and you know it, Marlie Simms.

But take your day and your hike. We can talk about this later.''

Marlie was tempted to grab her luggage and check out of the hotel immediately, but she knew she would have to battle Caid to do it. Another moment of his persuasive gentleness, however, and she knew she would do something extremely silly.

Instead, she took her cue from generations of those faced with untenable situations. She fled.

And got as far as the lobby, packed with men in leather, studs and bandanas, all looking rough and extremely dangerous.

Out with the stargazers and in with the Hells Angels, she thought, threading her way gingerly through the beefy group. What about the Hotel Limpia's quiet charm had drawn this crowd? Thank goodness she had Caid with her.

Not that she needed him, of course. Anyone who worked in a big city high school could face down a bunch of bikers, she was sure.

Once on the hotel's wide front porch, she found at least thirty motorcycles of various brands and sizes parked neatly side by side in front of it. More bikers milled around beside them.

Dazzled by the morning sunlight bouncing off so much chrome, Marlie reached for her dark glasses as she left the porch, and headed for her SUV at the end of the row.

Caid Matthews was leaning against its left front fender.

It was too much.

''No,'' Marlie shouted. ''We're not a p-pair, Caid Matthews. Here.'' Snatching the feather from her pocket, she threw it at him, backing up as fast as she could.

In her panic, she wasn't quite sure which Caid she was talking to, but it didn't matter. "You can have the darn thing. I don't want it. I just want to go *h-home!*"

"Watch out, Marlie," Caid exclaimed, reaching for her, but it was too late.

She backed right into a handlebar, stumbling a little so that her whole weight pushed against it. Caid made a grab for her as the machine toppled sideways into the bike next to it.

With a small cry of astonishment, Marlie turned in his arms just in time to see the entire row of expensive machines slowly lean, one by one, into the other, each landing with a small crash.

When it was over, which seemed to take a lifetime, the Fort Davis town square settled into deafening silence.

"Oh," Marlie whispered.

"That about covers it," Caid replied.

The bikers staring at her said nothing at all.

Marlie straightened her shoulders. "Let me handle this," she said.

"I don't think so."

Before she knew it, Caid had her squarely in back of him.

"The lady apologizes," he said to the mass of beef and muscle nearest them.

The man wore leather wristbands and heavy biker boots, Marlie noticed. She swallowed.

"A slight misstep on her part," Caid continued genially to the crowd that had gathered. "Of course, if there's any damage to your machines, I'll be glad to pay for it.''

''But, Caid, you can't afford...''

Locked eye to eye with the leather-clad brick wall in front of him, he didn't pay the least attention to her.

Cowboys, she silently huffed. *Give me a break!*

When she moved, Caid thrust out a restraining arm, but she ducked under it so that she stood beside him.

''*I'll* pay for the damage,'' she said clearly. ''And I'm truly sorry if I broke your motorcycles.''

The behemoth nearest Caid chuckled. ''Tell you what, little lady,'' he said. ''You two join us for prayer services under the stars tonight and we'll call it even.''

Marlie gaped.

''We're the Pearly Gates Cycle Club out of Midland,'' the man continued, ''here for our annual rally. Since we're all ministers, we don't go to bed at night without prayer.'' He winked.

''One of the ranches up the road keeps a field open for us for just that purpose, so the more the merrier. And in case you're wondering,'' he added kindly to Marlie, ''our wives and families will be joining us, but most of them will come in cars.''

By this time Marlie felt that prayer might well be in order. ''Thank you,'' she replied. ''I'd like to come.''

''Prude Ranch?'' Caid asked.

The man nodded.

''Thought as much. We'll see you tonight. And again, our apologies for any inconvenience.''

As the crowd dispersed, Marlie and Caid stood silently beside her vehicle, watching as the bikers picked up their machines, many of them using their bandanas to tenderly wipe off dust and polish up chrome.

"Well, hell," Caid said finally.

Marlie chuckled. "Thank heaven not this time."

His eyebrow quirked. Then he reached into his shirt pocket. "You dropped something," he said, taking out her feather.

The peace of the moment shattered as Marlie remembered just who this man was and how dangerous he was to her. "You can have it. It's yours."

"Cutes, you don't lie worth a damn."

"What?" Marlie stared up at the man in astonishment. "What did you call me?"

He stared at her blankly. "I don't know. Cutes, I guess. Sorry. Did I offend you? But you are cute, Marlie Simms. I thought it the first time I saw you."

Marlie gave a brief thought to what she'd first noticed about him, and felt her cheeks warm.

Caid noticed, of course. "What?"

She shook her head. "Nothing. It's just that someone else calls me that sometimes. And no, I'm not offended, but you have to admit, 'beautiful,' 'gorgeous,' or 'stunning' sounds much better."

"Perfect names for you at the right place and time, I imagine," he replied smoothly. "But in West Texas on a summer's day, 'Cutes' fits you to a tee. Hard to beat perfection, wouldn't you say?"

The cowboy definitely knew how to turn a phrase, Marlie thought, wondering if she'd just received a compliment or a put-down.

But before she could respond, Caid handed her the blue feather.

"It's yours," he said. "Looks exactly like mine, but it's not. I see that now. Has a different something about it."

"But you…"

With an odd look on his face, Caid placed the feather in her breast pocket so that its top peeked out jauntily.

Marlie felt the heat of his fingertips right through her shirt.

Her breath caught, and for a long silent moment the two of them stood in the strong West Texas sunlight, not touching, but caught fast in a web of awareness.

"Well," she finally managed, and cleared her throat. "Guess I'll be going."

"My truck or yours?" Caid replied.

Marlie came to her senses with a thump. "Oh, no you don't. I've had enough of the Matthews boys for one day. I'll be going alone, thank you."

"There's only one Matthews boy, Marlie, and you're looking at him."

Folding his arms across his broad chest, Caid leaned casually against the door of her SUV. "Let me put it this way," he explained, far too softly. "We can stand here in the middle of the Pearly Gates Cycle Club and the rest of Fort Davis and discuss how the hell you know so much about my business with the bank and the real estate office, not to mention Waldo…"

A lifted brow silently asked how she liked that suggestion. "Or I can show you a mystery or two while you clear up a mystery or two for me. Take your pick.''

Marlie glared at him, but knew she was defeated. ''Move aside, Cowboy,'' she snarled. ''I'm driving.''

Chapter Eight

When Caid sent her his heart-stopping grin, Marlie's temper fizzled right out. She had to give him credit, though. He didn't gloat.

"Go back and get a swimsuit and a couple of towels," he said. "I have a few errands to run first."

She snorted. "Aren't you afraid I'll take off without you?"

"You can run, Cutes," Caid drawled, his eyes sparkling a devilish green, "but you can't hide. I know everyone in town. And by now, everyone in town knows I know you, what kind of vehicle you drive and where you're staying. But you can try," he added magnanimously.

"You're on," Marlie said. In seconds she'd hopped in her SUV, backed carefully away from the now-upright row of motorcycles and sped out of the square, heading south.

Spying him in her rearview mirror, she stuck an

arm out the window and waved at Caid, still standing where she'd left him.

He looked totally unconcerned as he waved back.

Perhaps that was why, once she was out of sight of the main drag, Marlie doubled back to the rear entrance of the hotel. Going up the outdoor staircase mostly used by service personnel, she returned to her room.

It was empty. At some time Caid had left and Marlie wondered if he'd seen the motorcycle debacle, wondered if he had seen her talking to…himself.

What kind of man had Caid once been, she wondered, gathering her swimsuit and a couple of towels, when the gentle, giving spirit who was her roommate was a part of the sexy hunk who challenged her at every turn?

But she knew the answer.

Dangerous. As dangerous as the two parts of him were now, each in its own but completely different way.

One Caid made her melt. The other made her burn. Both made her nervous, shivery inside, caught between attraction and the very real fear of being hurt if she didn't keep her heart firmly in her head where it belonged.

Today, however, she was getting out of Dodge, and in spite of his belief in small-town gossip, she didn't think Caid would find her. She would take back streets till she got to the highway. Once there, hers was just another of the many tourist vehicles.

Also, to all appearances, she'd headed south, the opposite direction to the state park that was her destination.

Fort Davis's unpaved back streets, however, must have been laid out on cow paths. Several times Marlie found herself going in circles or at a dead end. A couple of times, without being quite sure how it happened, she found herself not on the road, but in someone's drive.

Finally, however, she came to a stop sign, looked around and realized the paved surface in front of her was the highway to the state park. At last.

It was a gorgeous morning, she thought, turning into the parking area for the trail she wanted to take. Hot already, though. She'd wasted too much time in town.

Leaving her vehicle, she stood beside it a moment to slather on sunscreen and sling the strap on her water bottle over her shoulder.

She had a foot propped on the front bumper and was retying the laces on her hiking boots when a decrepit pickup pulled into the parking space beside her.

"Howdy, Cutes," Caid said.

"You're late," Marlie replied, shading her eyes to look at him.

"Took me longer than I thought to borrow a pair of swim trunks."

Looking around at the rocky terrain, the various thorny plant life and a sky as purely blue as a madonna's mantle, Marlie couldn't quite control a smirk. A sign beside the trailhead warned hikers to carry plenty of water.

"Apparently great minds don't always think alike," she said. "I thought we would hike."

"Maybe." Caid still sat in Waldo's pickup, a beatup straw hat shading his eyes. "Maybe not." It was his turn to smirk. "But you went back for your suit, didn't you?"

"Maybe," Marlie replied defensively. "How do you know?"

"Steffie told me she saw you leaving the hotel with one rolled towel and another one slung over your shoulder."

Marlie looked at him, waiting.

"Steffie is Martin's wife. Martin and I played football together in high school. She works at the hotel. And Raul saw you pull out beside his station to get on the highway, in case that was your next question. After that, it was simple deduction, Watson."

"I'm slow today, Sherlock. Deduce, please."

"The state park is the only place with public trails on this particular highway," Caid replied blandly. "And you were carrying a water bottle and wearing hiking boots when you left this morning."

"Ah."

"Good plan, though, cutting through the back roads like you did."

Marlie laughed.

"You backed out of Roger Evans's driveway."

She laughed again. "All right, all right. You've definitely proved small-town gossip is faster than e-mail. So," she asked innocently, "are you ready to hike?"

Caid Matthews wasn't the only one observant. Unless he'd also borrowed a more serviceable pair of shoes, the cowboy was wearing boots—the kind made for riding, not doing the horse work himself. Most cowboys didn't like to walk.

This one looked chagrined for a moment, but got out of the truck.

"Right," he said, but she could tell he was deliberately avoiding looking at his boots. "I, uh, didn't bring a canteen."

"That's all right. I keep extra gear in the back and can fish one out for you," Marlie told him.

Without looking, she knew that his eyebrow quirked.

Just to keep Caid from getting too full of himself, she waited until they'd filled the extra water bottle at the public spigot and actually walked a good ways down the rough trail before she took mercy on him.

It *was* hot.

"Just where were you planning on swimming, Caid?" She deliberately didn't mention the other reason he'd insisted on coming with her this morning.

He grinned, but kept his strides matching hers as they both continued steadily along the rocky path. "Are you giving up, Cutes?"

"Maybe. Are you?"

"Absolutely. You still gonna drive?"

"Absolutely."

When she stopped, Caid stopped with her. "Hallelujah. Waldo's truck doesn't have air conditioning and it probably hasn't had shocks in twenty years."

Marlie laughed. Unlike Nicholas, Caid Matthews was an easy man to laugh with. "Not getting soft, are you?"

"Who, me?" He pressed a hand to his chest, pretending to be wounded. "Here I am, fresh out of the hospital and you ask a question like that?"

She froze. "Oh, Caid, I'm so sorry. I'd completely

forgotten. Of course you should get out of this hot sun. What was I thinking? But you've been so perky the last few days that I never thought..."

He stopped her simply by touching her cheek. "I'm fine, Marlie. I was teasing you, that's all."

And just like that, the spark Marlie had come to dread crackled between them again. The man had only to touch her, she thought dazedly, her gaze caught fast with his, and she went off like a Roman candle.

But it was Caid who slowly withdrew his fingers from her cheek, though just for a moment she felt the barest touch on her bottom lip.

"We need to talk," he said, and turned to lead the way back up the trail to the parking area.

What the hell was going on here? Caid wondered as he avoided a nasty piece of catclaw. The object was to charm this woman, not be charmed by her.

Marlie Simms knew far too much about his personal business, things no one knew except himself and Miles Durig at the bank. Even then, Durig didn't know of his plans to talk Waldo into retiring. No one did.

Cancel that. Cute little Marlie Simms obviously did.

And by golly, he was going to find out how.

Yet here he was, playing with her. Had been all morning, ever since she knocked over the row of motorcycles and was all set, if necessary, to join him in a free-for-all with the Hells Angels.

He'd been all set to kiss her, then and there...and

every moment since. A moment ago, he'd come damn close to doing just that.

And not because he wanted information, either. The only thing that had stopped him from kissing the woman senseless was the niggling thought of somehow hurting her by doing so. She was a nice girl.

Caid snorted.

"You say something?" Marlie asked, following behind him where the trail narrowed.

"No."

Nice girl, hah! Like Mata Hari was a nice girl. Marlie Simms was a spy. Had to be. But who was she spying for? And why?

Well, even if it meant kissing her right down to her cute little toes, Caid was going to find out. A tough job, but somebody had to do it.

After all, he'd lost his softer side, hadn't he?

So what if Marlie got hurt? At the next opportunity, he'd be friendly. *Real* friendly.

Bond, aka 007, seemed to make a point of it with his women, if Caid remembered his thrillers correctly.

His eyebrow quirked. Good one. Shame he couldn't share it with Marlie.

Marlie found herself driving on the same highway she'd driven into Fort Davis over a week ago. In daylight, it was as winding as it was in darkness, but now she saw that the scenery was breathtaking.

The highway wound through Limpia Canyon as it followed the tree-lined Limpia Creek, given its name by early Spanish explorers, Caid told her. On either side, looking like giant red ladyfingers, huge rock palisades walled its depth.

"And to think I missed all this," Marlie exclaimed, keeping one eye on her driving and the other on the beauty around and above her.

"It's pretty," Caid acknowledged, "but not easy to drive at night, if you're unfamiliar with the road. Why did you come in so late?"

"Stupidity on my part," Marlie replied. "I should have stopped at a motel on the interstate."

"Why didn't you?"

"I—I don't really know. Just wanted to get where I was going, I suppose. Actually, I'd planned on arriving in Fort Davis much earlier, but I stopped by my grandmother's in San Antonio to tell her goodbye. She had things she wanted me to do for her before I left, though, then insisted I have lunch with her. One thing led to another, and it was later than I'd planned on leaving town."

"Ah. The grandmother who is part Native American and knows about blue feathers," Caid said casually. "Tell me about her."

Marlie shot him a look. That last statement carried a touch of command in its tone.

But the cowboy sat at his ease, seemingly absorbed by the passing scenery out his window. Just making conversation, she supposed.

"Grammie says she's a member of the Iq'nata tribe," she replied with a smile.

"Never heard of them."

"Not many have. According to my grandmother, early in the last century, tiny remnants of several Native American nations created their own tribe, the Iq'nata, to keep their customs and beliefs from dying out completely. To avoid drawing attention to themselves, they deliberately blended into the American culture. Grammie takes pride in the fact that anthropologists don't seem to know they exist.''

"Interesting. Are you, too, a member of the tribe?''

"No. Someday, perhaps. You have to be born into it, but in addition, you have to be chosen. Very few are. That's how the tribe stays out of the mainstream.''

"So who does the choosing?'' Caid asked.

"You'll laugh.''

"No I won't. Scout's honor.'' He held up three fingers and looked solemn, though Marlie could see the gleam in his green eyes.

"The Great Ones.''

"Beg pardon?''

"The Great Ones do the choosing. Actually, I'm not sure if the Great Ones are gods, spirits or real live people. Grammie says you have to be a member of the tribe to know that part. Still, when the Great Ones speak, Grammie listens and passes along what they tell her.''

"Signs in the heavens and portents in feathers, hmm?''

Marlie didn't like the note of skepticism in Caid's voice that made Grammie sound like a charlatan in a tattered shawl reading tea leaves at five bucks a pop.

"My grandmother,'' she replied, keeping her voice even, "has a Ph.D. in physics *and* philosophy, *and* teaches at the University in San Antonio. It is her belief that physics and spirituality will irrefutably collide in the near future, and she wants to be there when they do.''

"Wow. Sounds like quite a woman.''

"She is." But Marlie had to be fair. "My family has a saying though. 'When you're going on a trip, never accept one of Gram's little presents if she didn't buy it.'"

"Or?"

"Or you never know what or who the Great Ones will hook up with you. Believe me, strange things happen in my family when Grammie gives a gift she didn't buy in a store."

"That bad, huh?"

Marlie nodded. "But she didn't *give* me the feather. She just pointed it out to me. It was on the pavement beside the door of my car when I left her house."

"Technically not a gift, I suppose."

"Lord, I hope not," Marlie replied fervently. "Or I would never have picked it up."

"But you did, and now you carry it in your pocket," Caid pointed out. Then added the clincher, "A jay feather that looks just like mine, right down to the small black dot at its base."

"Coincidence," Marlie said.

"You don't want to be my very good friend, I can tell," he said teasingly. "Or is that really what Grammie said?"

Time to change the subject.

"Where did you get *your* feather and why is it lucky?" she asked brightly.

He shot her a look. "Long story."

"Long drive."

"I told you that Waldo packed me down off a mountain when I broke my leg, I believe."

"Um-hmm." He hadn't. It was the other Caid who told her, but she let it go.

"I was alone in some pretty rough country when for no apparent reason, a blue jay flew right at me squawking and carrying on. Startled me, startled my horse. The upshot was, I got thrown, my horse bolted and I was on the ground with a broken leg with no one knowing where I was."

"And you call that a *lucky* feather?"

"I'm getting to that. Along came Waldo. How he knew I was in trouble, I'll never know. Maybe because that jay was still sitting in a tree having a noise fit. One of its feathers lay not too far from me. Waldo told me to keep it. It was a good luck sign, he said. As you can imagine, I didn't quite see it that way."

So Waldo, too, believed in signs, Marlie thought. Yet after her conversation with him, she wasn't surprised.

"Just to be on the safe side, Waldo scouted the area before we left and found cougar sign on up the trail, including the tracks of a couple of little ones. Instead of just a broken leg, if I'd kept going I could have been dead meat. I've worn that feather in my hat ever since."

He took her, or she took him, to the huge spring-fed pool in Balhorhea. There they splashed and played and dunked each other as if they'd known each other all their lives.

Surrounded by at least a hundred others determined to beat the West Texas heat, they seemed to exist in a world of their own, Caid thought, as they returned to Fort Davis by the same route they'd come.

Yet he damn well *hadn't* known this woman all his life, however comfortable she was to be with, or he wouldn't have had the fun of discovering so many things about her.

He'd discovered, for instance, that Marlie could swim with the joie de vivre of a dolphin. And that she had a sister who was a nurse and a brother who was a marine. She had a passion for Fudgesicles and a fear of water spiders.

And, he'd learned, on her a simple one-piece bathing suit with modest cleavage could set off a derriere to make a strong man weep. Not to mention her great legs.

All day, juicy nuggets of discovery about this sprite of a woman only added to her appeal. And the more he found out, the more he wanted to know.

Like how the hell she knew so damned much about *him,* for instance.

To his amazement, with almost no prodding on his part, Marlie had lived up to the promise of her clear gray eyes and revealed her knowledge of him casually, as if she took for granted that he knew that she knew.

She knew he'd once actually owned a horse named Old Paint, for instance. And that he'd gone to university, but dropped out his senior year when his father died.

She knew his mother and father were dead, and that his father had built their ranch house to his mother's design.

But what really gave him the willies, Caid thought, was that she was seemingly aware of far more than just facts.

In some strange, petrifying way, he could sense her complete understanding of how much he still missed his mother, even after all these years. And without ever actually saying it, she seemed to know that though he'd respected his father, it was Waldo who'd heard his childish confessions.

Anyone in Fort Davis could have given her basic facts about the Matthews family. That was a given. But no one but himself knew his deeper emotions. Not even to Janice had he bared his soul.

Marlie Simms, however, seemed to have a more than nodding acquaintance with it.

"I want my mystery," she said suddenly, neatly passing a slower moving vehicle.

Caid, lost in thought, caught a startled breath, then chuckled silently. Good one, and she didn't even know it.

"You promised," she added.

"And I forgot. Sorry, Cutes. Good thing we're close. Next gate on the right, turn in."

He got permission from the Chandlers, then directed Marlie down a ranch road that followed the fence line. When they came to a shallow dip, he had her stop.

"Here we are," he said, and got out.

Marlie left the SUV to stand beside him. "Yep, here we are," she mimicked.

"You're not impressed at all, are you, Cutes?"

"Why, certainly. It's beautiful country. Deep healthy grass. Rain this year, I take it?"

He nodded.

"Lots of wide blue sky. No rain tonight?"

He shook his head.

"Cows in the distance. A few cottonwoods in that draw over there. Stone fencing."

"Bingo."

"Cows, cottonwoods or stone fencing?"

"It might not be fencing," Caid replied, keeping his tone enigmatic and enjoying himself hugely.

He'd only introduced this "mystery" this morning as a way of getting Marlie off to himself, but he had to admit, she knew how to take something marginally interesting, at best, and make it downright fun.

"Oh?"

"That's right. No one's quite sure who built the walls. There are several of them scattered around these parts, but they don't really fence anything. And if you look closely, they're made of rocks piled together but nicely fitted. No mortar."

"The West Texas version of Machu Picchu, you say?"

He grinned at her. "Not quite. For one thing, they probably date only to the eighteen hundreds."

"So what's the mystery?"

"The mystery is why anyone would bother to build anything so labor intensive that performs no discernible function," Caid replied. "Any ideas?"

"None. What does popular wisdom say?"

"Well," he drawled, "Some think the commanding officer at the fort ordered the soldiers to build them to keep the men occupied when they weren't chasing Indians. But that's just speculation."

She laughed. "The historical equivalent of digging a hole and filling it in. I think the army still does it."

"Hard to dig holes in West Texas rock," Caid answered with a shrug.

Marlie thought of the cowboy's stubborn hard-headedness. "I've noticed."

Before they went back to the state park to get Waldo's truck, Caid took Marlie to dinner at the local Mexican restaurant. It didn't matter that she was wearing the same clothes she'd been in all day, he told her. It wasn't that kind of place.

By this time, however, Marlie was starting to worry about Caid at the hotel. It was already getting dark and she'd been out all day. With the enormous Matthews' appetite, he was probably starving by now.

She must have revealed her unease because Caid touched her hand to halt her tearing to shreds the paper napkin wrapped around the knife and fork.

"What?" he asked quietly. "Never mind. You're worried about your...roommate, aren't you?"

Marlie nodded, amazed that he could be so perceptive.

"So we'll take him a takeout," Caid said. "No big deal. Anything else?"

"No, but thank you. Ca—I mean he, uh, doesn't do restaurants."

Caid leaned comfortably against the padded back of the booth where they were seated, but for no reason at all Marlie suddenly felt like the fly in the parlor of the spider.

"This roommate," he said softly. "Is he ugly? Badly scarred, perhaps? Or just shy? No one seems to have seen him but you."

"How do you know?" she asked tartly.

But the ironic lift of an eyebrow said it all. Small town.

"He's not ugly," she said, knowing she had to say something, preferably something true, since her face made lying extremely difficult. "He—he was involved in an accident, and since then gets nervous in crowded places."

"Which, in a place like Fort Davis, makes everyone curious as hell. If he wants to hide, he should do it in a city," Caid noted sardonically.

"Maybe he's not wanting to hide," Marlie told him, frowning. "Maybe this situation is as foreign to him as it would be to…to you. Maybe until he can figure out what's going on, he just doesn't want company."

"Except you."

"Except me. But I'm going home soon, and then everyone is on their own," she said, glaring at the man across from her to show that she meant it.

"Planning to leave your, um, roommate here, are you?" Caid asked, his tone bland.

Like good salsa was bland, Marlie thought. "Definitely. And I'm not taking home any souvenirs."

"Local boy?"

"You might say that." The term "boy" wouldn't come close to a description of Caid Matthews, however.

The waitress set tortilla soup in front of them, and Caid used his spoon to scoop a string of melted Monterey Jack off a piece of avocado. "The plot thickens," he replied.

He insisted they take "her roommate" his supper before returning to the state park. "Can't have the man go hungry," he said cheerfully.

For her part, Marlie wasn't enthused about seeing Caid at the hotel only to tell him she was going out again. Why this should be the case, she didn't know.

In spite of his assertion this morning, they weren't a pair. They couldn't be. He had to know it. Why, the man had never even tried to kiss her, beyond the one time out at his ranch. Such reticence didn't sound like a man in love.

Marlie blinked. Where had that thought come from? Of course, Caid wasn't in love, and neither was she.

For one thing, after so short a time, she couldn't possibly be over…over…whatshisname. Her used-to-be fiancé.

Nicholas, that was the name! How could she have forgotten it?

The truth was, however, that she couldn't even re-member what Nicholas looked like anymore. When she tried to conjure his image, all she saw was a wick-edly cocked eyebrow and eyes the color of pine nee-dles.

But that didn't mean she was in love with Caid, Marlie told herself staunchly. Either of him. It just meant she had a lot on her mind, that's all.

Quietly, she pushed open the door to her room at the Limpia. The room was dark, not even the televi-sion on. Was Caid asleep? But it was early yet. Surely not.

Even so, she felt around until she located a lamp, turning it on instead of the overhead light. In its dim glow, she saw that both beds were still made. No light shone under the bathroom door.

"Caid?" she called, just to make sure.

Placing the supper she'd brought him on the night-stand, she looked around the room restlessly. Where *was* he? From the looks of things, he'd been gone all day, just as she had. Was he all right? Had anything happened to him?

Then she saw the note on her bed pillow. "Back later," it said.

She sighed, with relief and maybe a touch of disappointment. Caid hadn't missed her apparently. Taking the note, she placed it on the pillow of *his* bed, leaving him the same message.

Caid was waiting for her in the lobby, talking to Ann. "Ready?" he asked, glancing at her sharply.

"Oh, lord," Marlie exclaimed. "I totally forgot. We have to go to church!"

Just as she knew it would, Caid's eyebrow quirked.

Ann merely looked curious. "Church?"

"Penance," Caid told her, "for playing dominoes with holy motorcycles this morning. Let's go, Cutes. We'll pray for you, Annie."

They arrived at the open field a few miles out of town just in time for a last hymn and the closing prayer. Starlight glistened off motorcycle handlebars, and now and then the scrunch of leather sounded like the low croak of a night frog.

"That was nice," Marlie said, once they were back in the SUV, headed, one more time, for the state park.

"Yeah. They do this every year," Caid replied.

"You knew those bikers," Marlie said accusingly, "and you let me think they were Hells Angels?"

"Well, I knew they weren't Angels, but I didn't know they were preachers," Caid defended himself. "Several biker groups rally in this area. Just because

they ride motorcycles doesn't mean they're all mean-
ies, you know. Still, even preachers can lose their
religion when someone plays fast and loose with their
pride and joy.''

"I didn't thank you for trying to protect me this
morning,'' Marlie said softly.

"My pleasure, Cutes, but it turned out you weren't
in any danger.''

"Maybe not, but you didn't know it for sure until
it was over. Here's your truck. You're going to have
a long drive back to the ranch.''

The parking area was pitch black, no lights anywhere to dim a night sky spangled with millions of
stars. Caid didn't move to get out but, as the motor
idled, sat quietly in the seat beside her, looking up at
them out the open window.

"Guess this is it,'' he said at last. Reaching over,
he turned off the motor.

"Now, Cutes, suppose you tell me how you know
more about my business than the IRS.''

Chapter Nine

Oh, Lord, Marlie thought.

They'd had such a good time today, she figured Caid had forgotten his suspicions. She should have known better. No-nonsense, get-to-the-point Caid Matthews wouldn't forget—or forgive—a thing.

So how was she going to explain to this Caid with the hard-edged personality that she'd been living with his gentler self since his run-in with a tree?

"I don't know what you're talking about," she replied innocently. Thank goodness it was dark. He wouldn't be able to see her lying face.

The interior of the SUV seemed to shrink, its atmosphere suddenly oppressive.

"I'll be more specific, then," Caid said, his voice a soft slither up the back of her neck.

Marlie swallowed.

"You knew I had an appointment with Miles Durig at the bank, an appointment I was unable to keep.

Confidential information, Cutes. Is someone at the bank carrying tales out of school, by any chance?''

She licked her lips.

But had Caid inadvertently given her an out? Could she perhaps claim small-town gossip as her source? Yet he had to know such information wasn't circulating freely. ''Um, not that I know of.''

He waited.

''I don't know anyone at the bank,'' Marlie added brightly, relieved that she could tell the literal truth, about this at least.

He waited.

''I, uh, just heard it somewhere. At The Drugstore perhaps, or at the fort.''

He waited.

''Oh, all right!'' she finally burst out, knowing she was cornered and by now ready to sing for her life and be done with it. ''*You* told me, darn it!''

''Unh-huh, I didn't.''

''Uh-huh, you did. You told me about the Rolling M's financial difficulties and how you planned to ask the bank for a loan against the sale of five hundred acres. *And* you told me you planned to ask Waldo to retire soon because you needed to save his salary.''

Caid sat utterly still, but Marlie didn't care. She was tired of holding it in, tired of walking a tightrope of half lies and innuendo.

''I know all sorts of things about you, Caid Matthews,'' she added on a quieter note, ''and you told it all to me yourself. If secrets have been spilled, you have only yourself to blame.''

Oppressive silence became a third party in the vehicle. Through the open windows, the outside darkness was equally mute, not even a night creature rustling among the cacti. Around and above, a multitude of stars shone a symphony of twinkling points heard only by the eye.

"What else do you know?" Caid asked at last.

And Marlie told him. If the man didn't believe her, too bad. His loss. And, she thought sadly, a big one.

"I know you're a neatnik. You hang up your clothes at night and never leave dirty socks lying around. You're allergic to the scent of lavender," she said, "and have a sneeze like the horn of a cruise ship leaving port."

"Everyone in Jeff Davis County knows it, too. Tell me something no one knows but me, Marlie. And you, of course," he added with a touch of sarcasm.

Marlie gripped the steering wheel in front of her and stared out the windshield into the night's dark purity. "All right. Here's what I know that no one but you knows, and now myself." She took a deep breath.

"I know," she said quietly, "what you were thinking at the moment you hit the tree."

Caid huffed a short clipped laugh. "No, you don't. And besides, how can you prove it? I've forgotten myself."

"Yes, Caid, I do. And I don't have to prove it. You can, because you remember it very clearly."

Abruptly, Caid opened the door to the SUV, making her jump, but he merely walked around its hood, his boots crunching over the rocky ground in the silence. Once on her side of the vehicle, he leaned negligently against it, his lower back braced against the front fender near Marlie's door.

In the distance, a bird called sleepily. Another answered. A rising sickle moon barely peeped over the dark jagged horizon.

"So tell me what I was thinking, Marlie Simms."

Marlie was in no mood to be intimidated. Besides, after bunking with him for a week, she knew the cowboy far too well. Today had been fun, but not necessarily a revelation.

"You were fighting with yourself," she told him evenly. "*You* knew that you had to sell five hundred acres in order to save your ranch, but your heart was adamantly opposed to it, telling you that no one in the ranch's history had ever sold so much as a single boulder."

She paused. "Driving back to Fort Davis that evening, you were literally a man at war with himself, half of you knowing what had to be done, the other half protesting with every breath. Am I right so far?"

"Maybe," he replied grudgingly.

"Asking Waldo to retire in order to free up his salary was also imperative, you thought. But there was that heart of yours again, that gentle side of you who loves Waldo like a father, raging against such a cruel act and calling you all sorts of vile names."

"Perhaps."

"So there you were in the truck, fighting with yourself the way you'd been for weeks, half of you knowing you had to be practical, half of you knowing that to be practical might destroy an old man, and most certainly would reduce the property that, against great odds, your family had fought for three generations to keep."

Caid didn't speak, and Marlie, too, left the truck to

lean against it beside him. Though they didn't touch, she could feel his warmth, and feel the sadness in him.

"Out jumped a deer," she continued, keeping her voice low but knowing she had to carry this through to the end, "and a ponderosa pine met its maker. You almost did, too. Half of you wound up in the hospital, and half of you...well, half of you didn't."

"It's far-fetched, but a good story so far, Cutes," Caid said into the silence, his own voice as normal as flowers in May. "So tell me, which half didn't go to the hospital?"

"Guess," Marlie replied, stung. She should have known. Both Caids absolutely refused to take their breakup seriously.

"I'll give you a hint, though," she added tartly, "since for an intelligent man you've become suddenly obtuse. Do you still have reservations about selling a corner of the Rolling M?"

"Nah. It has to be done. I don't have a problem with it anymore. Might not be something I want to do, but that's the way life goes sometimes."

"Here's another hint. What have you decided to do about Waldo?"

"I love the man, but he's eighty-three, Cutes. He has a good pension coming, so money will never be a problem for him. The problem is finding money for the ranch. I think Waldo will understand."

"So, Caid," Marlie asked sarcastically, "which half of you didn't go to the hospital?"

The sickle moon had risen higher now and Marlie had enough light to see a gleam that was probably Caid's grin.

"Must have been the wimpy half, Cutes. Is that the answer you're looking for? Just don't expect me to regret it. If you're waiting for some great psychological breakthrough on my part, you're plain out of luck. You counselors should save your degree for high school students."

"Oh?" Marlie replied, glancing at Caid's dark profile from the corner of her eye. "How do you know I'm a high school counselor?"

He shifted. "You...told me? That is, you told me."

"You're right, I did. Do you remember when?"

"Today," Caid answered quickly. "We talked a lot today. I think you mentioned a problem with your job."

"No," Marlie replied, "We didn't talk about my job at all today. I told you about my grandmother, if you recall. We discussed my problem with Marcia on the day you got out of the hospital."

"Couldn't be. I distinctly remember discussing the whereabouts of my hat on the first day I met you. We sure didn't talk about anything personal that morning, especially not you almost getting fired."

"So when did we talk about it, Caid?"

"I don't know," he replied irritably. "You're a counselor and you got a bum deal. Your boss was an idiot, in my opinion, and your ex-boyfriend a real piece of rabbit droppings. But still, what difference does it make when we discussed the bozos?"

Marlie sighed. "Think about it, Caid, and I'm sure the answer to that will come to you."

Caid was quiet a good five minutes.

Beside him, Marlie enjoyed the peacefulness of the night and the subtle perfume of the high desert air.

She enjoyed more, however, the scent of warm sunshine coming from Caid.

He stood loosely, leaning slightly against her, arms crossed over his chest, his head bowed as if in deep thought.

Against her? Good grief! Somehow the inches between them had disappeared, and the side of Caid's body now joined hers, shoulder to ankle.

How, she wondered, had that happened?

"Well, hell," Caid said. "Damned if I know."

Marlie jumped, startled. Could the man read her mind?

"I just remember you telling me, that's all," he added, and she realized with relief that his thoughts were still a subject or two behind hers.

"Something else I remember," he added softly, turning to face her.

For no reason at all, Marlie's heart rolled over. "What?" she asked, not looking at him.

"I remember how much I wanted to kiss you when you told me about that girl," he said gruffly, "and being too stupid to do it."

"Oh," she exhaled, and then didn't breathe at all for a while.

She remembered, too, she thought hazily as Caid's mouth plundered hers. His mouth. Oh, his mouth. She could drink from it all day.

And she remembered his hands. Threaded through her hair, touching her face, a rough thumb tracing the bone beneath her eyes, exploring the curvature of her mouth.

Such a sweet, sweet kiss, standing beside her SUV

on a hot West Texas afternoon. She'd said goodbye that day.

But she didn't…oh, lordy, what was he doing? She didn't remember his hands slowly sliding down her back to spread across the fullness of her hips, leaving havoc in their wake. And she didn't remember them coming up under her breasts, seeking, finding, tantalizing her body into mindless sensitivity.

This was all wonderfully new, but she would remember it until the day she died.

She would remember, too, the feel of Caid's hair slipping crisply through her fingers at his nape. She would remember the warm bristles on his cheek, the column of his throat as she traced it with her tongue to the hollow between his ear and his jaw line.

And she would never forget his soft startled gasp when she did it.

Caid, she thought bemusedly. Caid. But more Caid than she'd ever known.

When he deepened the kiss, she met him halfway, straining upward, opening her mouth to his seeking tongue, seeking more of him, seeking more….

And realized at some self-preserving level, that this practiced lover had no more.

As if aware of her sudden distress, Caid slowly broke the kiss, pulling away slightly to rest his forehead against hers, his breathing ragged.

With her knees gone to gelatin, the only thing keeping Marlie standing was Caid's forehead against her own and his arms lightly embracing her shoulders.

"Well, hell," Caid whispered.

Marlie laughed shakily. It beat the alternative. "Deep subject." She, too, whispered.

"Old one, Cutes. You can do better than that." The hand that brushed her jaw as he lifted his head had a faint tremor to it.

She cleared her throat, hoping she could speak normally. "How about this one. Let me put a damper on things."

"Fire away."

In spite of what she was about to introduce, the corner of Marlie's mouth twitched. But she sobered immediately.

"You have a question or two to ask me," she said.

The two of them again stood shoulder to shoulder, leaning against the SUV, but leaning slightly against each other, too. She felt Caid's sigh more than heard it.

"Guess so."

But he didn't ask them right away. Instead he pointed out a satellite, arcing overhead like a star with a mission. And then he showed her the great flow of the Milky Way and pointed out its center.

Then with no change at all in his voice, he said, "I'll agree that you knew what I was thinking when I hit the tree. But how could you know it when I'm positive that I didn't tell you?"

"You're not all that positive," Marlie replied dryly. "And I think you know the answer already. But I'll spell it out for you, if you like, so that I'm the one who sounds one card shy of a full deck. Lord knows, after the last several days I ought to be used to it by now."

Caid draped a casual arm around her shoulder and instantly Marlie's growing hostility melted. This Caid could be almost as sweet as the other when he put his mind to it.

"The situation is just so bizarre, you know? How would you like to have your hotel room occupied by a ghost who isn't dead?"

"You mean a doppelgänger?"

"Yes, that's it! I couldn't think of the word, but I'm not sure of its specific definition. Whatever. If that's what it is, it's you, Caid."

He laughed. "I don't think so. The concept is European, or something. Can you imagine a West Texas cowpoke with his own ghost walking around?"

"Yes," she replied, "I can. And so can you. Stop trying to play games with yourself. You know that your personality wasn't the same after you had the accident. You said it yourself. Well, where did that piece of you that's missing go when you went to the hospital?"

But she didn't give him time to answer.

"It—*you*—went to the Hotel Limpia, to the room you planned to stay in so you could get to the bank early the next morning. But since no one could see you or hear you and everyone thought you were in the hospital, Ann was kind enough to let me have it that night when there wasn't another one to be had."

"This is the craziest thing I've ever heard, Cutes," Caid said flatly.

"Definitely."

Neither spoke for a long moment, but they leaned even more into each other. Their sigh was in two part harmony.

"But you heard me. You saw me," Caid said at last.

"Heard you in the night. Saw you in the daylight."

"Like what you saw?"

She just *knew* he'd grinned.

"There!" Marlie exclaimed. "You did it again. You echo things from your other self, Caid. You know things I didn't tell you, but that I told him— you. Don't you see? You're not completely separated. There's bound to be a way to reconcile the two of you into one again."

"I don't think so."

"Sure there is, Caid. All you have to do is confront yourself."

"Maybe. But if what you say is true, Marlie, I don't want that side of me back. This is a tough world, calling for tough decisions. I can't be a bleeding heart every time something I have to do isn't comfortable for someone else or doesn't follow tradition."

He stepped away from her and Marlie almost toppled sideways, if Caid not reached out to steady her.

"Don't you get it?" he demanded, thrusting his hands into his back pockets. "I'm better off without the side of me that makes decisions based on emotions. Hell, I married a woman because I thought I was in love with her when all she wanted was my ranch. I've worked a man far past the time when he should be taking it easy and called it *love*."

In the faint light of starshine, Marlie saw him turn his face away from her so that he could stare into the night at the rugged land of his birth.

"Love is for fools, Marlie," he told her softly. "Anyone who says love is a kindness has never seen it destroy everything they hold dear."

"It doesn't have to be that way, Caid."

"Maybe not. But for me, it does. Now come here, Cutes, and let me show you the Big Dipper."

With Marlie standing in front of him, he stood behind her to place one hand on her shoulder and point with the other, then he swiveled her a bit.

"And see that big bright star over there looking important?"

"Hard to miss."

"That's not a star at all. It's Venus. You, Cutes. Did I tell you what a stunner you are in a bathing suit?"

She laughed, pleased. Whatshisname's compliments had been so rare, Marlie had about decided she had nothing to be complimented on.

"Thanks. You're not so bad yourself," she replied.

Caid chuckled. "Guess that makes us a handsome pair."

Another echo. Marlie wanted to weep.

One Caid spoke of paired hearts, she thought morosely, but this Caid, the one who lit fires with his kisses, the one who ignited her libido in a way no one ever had before, was only talking bodies.

Yet somehow he had turned her to face him, and somehow her mouth was meeting his again with the exuberance of an old friend, and somehow she was clinging to him as if he were a liferaft in a sea of sharks.

It wasn't enough that she was half in love with the man's ghost. She had this man's shirt half unbuttoned.

Was she certifiably crazy?

With an effort, Marlie tore herself away, breathing heavily.

"Well, hell," Caid said, sounding ragged himself.

"Definitely."

He stilled. "That bad?"

"That good. You're, um, a very good kisser. But I don't want to be your summer fling, Caid."

"You know I have nothing else to offer," he replied quietly. "But I really…like you, and we get along pretty good together, wouldn't you say?"

"Don't we just. But I'm going home."

"Not home. To the hotel," he said quickly. "You're right. It's late." And opening the door, he hustled her into her SUV.

"About my hat," he added, his tone diffident as she started the motor. "Do you think you could get it back for me? I miss it."

Yes, Marlie thought sadly, *I imagine you do.*

"I'll try," she said aloud. "But I can't make any promises."

"Good enough. I'll call you tomorrow. Drive carefully going back."

"I'm not the one who runs into innocent trees," Marlie retorted. "*You* drive carefully, Caid Matthews. I want you in one piece."

Caid's eyebrow didn't quirk.

Good one, she thought. Too bad the man refused to appreciate it.

Chapter Ten

Marlie let herself into the hotel. The lobby was quiet, except for a few bikers, looking odd in their leathers as they sat casually with their wives or children in the hotel's Victorian parlor.

One or two of them waved to her, and she waved back before starting slowly up the stairs to her room. Hard to believe that only this morning she'd begun the day by knocking over a row of motorcycles.

It seemed a lifetime ago.

But every day she spent with either of the Caids seemed a lifetime, packed as they were with laughter and sorrow, the hours chock-full of drama and slapstick. She didn't know whether to laugh or weep.

"What are you doing, coming in so late, Cutes?"

She jumped, startled. Caid was coming up the stairs just behind her.

"*Me?*" she replied accusingly.

Ann looked up at her curiously from the desk near the foot of the stairs.

With a weak smile, Marlie waggled her fingers and tried to look nonchalant while picking up the pace, hoping she didn't look like she was running.

Caid kept up with her. "What's the hurry, Cutes?"

"Everyone in town thinks I talk to myself, that's the hurry," she growled softly, knowing she made no sense at all. "Where have you *been?* Do you know how late it is?"

It was difficult being irate in a whisper.

"Yeah, it's time for the ten-o'clock news." He used his key to open the room. "I like it when you sound like a nagging wife," he added.

Marlie, coming through the door, gaped at him. "Are you out of your mind?"

"Definitely. I plan to stay that way." He tossed his hat so that it snagged a decorative prong on the dresser mirror, the blue feather flashing as it sailed through the air. "Now, what has you in such a tizzy?"

"You," Marlie replied baldly. "Doesn't it bother you the least little bit that no one can see you or hear you, Caid? Don't you want your life back?"

And just like that, all of Caid's good-humored nonchalance disappeared.

"I'm supposed to want a life where the man who packed me off a mountain when I broke my leg is forced into retirement like he doesn't have value anymore?" Caid asked bitterly, turning on her.

"I'm supposed to love a life where my father and grandfather and his father before him are probably spinning in their graves because a part of the original homestead is being sold, probably to some developer who'll carve it into quarter-acre lots?"

He jammed his fingers through his hair, making it stick up at wild angles.

"Hell no, I don't want my life back, Marlie. And no, it doesn't bother me that no one can see me or hear me. Not anymore. I'm too damned ashamed of what that bastard has become. Besides, you can see me just fine, and hear me, too."

Walking to the dresser, Caid retrieved his hat from where he'd just tossed it and gazed for a long moment at the blue feather.

Then he came toward her, hat in hand, but with his green-eyed gaze holding hers so that she was unable to look away.

Reaching out, he took the feather peeking out of her breast pocket and tucked it beside its mate in the hatband, one now the twin of the other. He placed the hat on Marlie's head.

"You make me the only person I want to be, Marlie Simms."

All the pent-up frustrations of the day found an outlet at last. There was no holding back the tears streaming down Marlie's cheeks.

Caid took her into his arms.

"Oh, Caid, you mustn't say such things," she whispered wetly.

But she put her head on his broad shoulder, just as, with one or the other of him, she'd done so many times over the past several days.

It took a while for her to whuffle and sniff and hiccup her way into a semblance of togetherness, but all the while Caid held her close, gently rubbing his hands over her back and shoulders and making soothing noises low in his throat.

Finally, she lifted her head and he handed her his huge handkerchief so she could blow her nose. Once she'd honked into it, she put her head back on his shoulder, emotionally spent.

"I love you, Marlie."

Her head snapped up again. "You can't!"

"I can," he said flatly, "and I do. And I think you love me, too."

Marlie stilled, caught by what she saw in Caid's eyes. When faced with a bared heart's pure honesty, nothing less than honesty can be returned, she thought sadly.

"I think so, too," she said.

He kissed her then, a kiss of such unadulterated passion that she would have wept again, had not all her tears been spent.

Twice she'd experienced this man's passion tonight, she thought hazily. At the park, his kisses had taught her body to sing, to reach high notes she'd never known were in her. But in his kiss now was the kind of heart's passion that creates symphonies.

As Marlie sank into the exquisite beauty of Caid's mouth on hers, she knew for the first time a love originating before life began and one that would live long after it was gone.

No wonder she'd been able to see and hear him when no one else could, she thought as the universe itself hummed around her. Her soul, her deepest spirit, was linked to that of this one man.

Just as the Great Ones had known.

Pulling her mouth from his, she stepped out of Caid's embrace.

In this time and in this place, such love was not for her.

And because Caid loved her, he allowed it.

"What is there about 'I love you' that you don't like?" he asked quietly.

"Oh, Caid, nothing at all, I promise you. I have no words for the wonderful gift you have just given me. It's just that…I—I'm awful. I know it."

She took his hat off her head and handed it to him.

"I want more," she whispered miserably.

"Hush," he said. "You're being too hard on yourself, Cutes, and I won't have it. You're not awful. Just tell me what more you want."

"You already know, Caid. I know you do." She dropped her lashes for a moment but lifted them again almost immediately.

"I want what goes beyond kisses," she said, her eyes meeting his own with that clear direct gaze he so loved about her. "I not only want love, I want a lover. I want hot, sweaty sex and X-rated tumbles in the hay. And I want children."

Leave it to Marlie to have the courage to address what he'd been willing to evade, Caid thought, as her words set up a longing in him that almost made him sick to his stomach.

For whatever reason, he could do everything with this woman that a normal man could—hold her, kiss her, play with her. Everything but what he most wanted to do. And she knew it.

"I'm sorry, Cutes," he said finally, with a small sigh.

"Don't be. It's not your fault."

"It isn't?"

"Of course it isn't. You're the heart of you, Caid. Don't you see? And at heart, everyone with any sense knows that sex and love are not synonymous. My heart knows it, too," she added softly, "but my body is a whole other story."

Caid couldn't help himself. Tossing the hat he still held onto his bed, he reached out and pulled Marlie back into his arms where she belonged. Her silken head homed to his shoulder and he cupped the back of it, threading his fingers through her short curls.

He couldn't give her the more that she wanted, he thought sadly, but he could at least give her comfort.

Their sigh was in two-part harmony.

Caid thought his heart might rip in two. He'd known for a long time that it was his pride, not his heart, that was hurt when Janice left, he thought.

But to lose Marlie....

Even worse was Marlie's anguish. He felt it to the tips of his boots.

Unable to bear it any longer, he finally murmured huskily, "Toss you for first shower."

As he'd hoped, she looked up and grinned at him. But before she could say a word, he lifted her up and tossed her, squealing, onto her bed, where she bounced on her rump a couple of times.

"Tails, I win," he said.

Marlie threw a pillow at him. "You cheated!" Then she threw the other one.

Your Cheating Heart. Caid knew the moment the old Hank Williams tune flowed through her mind.

He cocked an eyebrow. "Good one," he said.

* * *

When Marlie got out of the bathroom, Caid was sitting up in bed, looking far handsomer than he had a right to with the dark hair on his bare chest arrowing down enticingly to the sheet pulled low at his waist. What she wouldn't give to crawl into the bed with him.

And why not? she asked herself. It wasn't as if she wouldn't be safe. This Caid was so...so comforting. To sleep in his arms would melt away her troubles.

But her troubles were not what she wanted melted. And she darn sure didn't want to be safe. To lie with him would be hell. Just like not lying with him was going to be.

She crawled into bed. Her own.

"So tell me what you did today," she said.

Darn it, why did Caid have to sleep in the nude? But if she looked straight ahead, she wouldn't be able to see him, lying in the other bed with all his glory under the sheet.

"Went exploring with the movie company," he answered. "Talk about people willing to throw money around."

Marlie examined a painting of voluptuous roses on the far wall. "How did you wind up with them?"

He laughed. "Hitched a ride. They were standing on the curb talking when I walked by, and I heard them mention Yance Chisolm's name, so I stopped to eavesdrop. Seems the C3 has some acreage they wanted to look at. Well hell, they'd left the door to their vehicle open. Looked like an invitation to me."

"And away you went," Marlie said with a chuckle. Her gaze traced the wallpaper pattern.

"It's been a while since I've been out that way,"

Caid replied, all innocence. "Yance showed 'em around some, and I just kinda tagged along, but the area Stephen and John were most interested in, Yance didn't want to lease, even when they offered him enough money to strangle a good-size heifer."

"Stephen and John?"

"The film fellas. Not bad sorts once you get to know them."

Marlie reached over and switched off the bedside lamp. "We can talk in the dark," she said.

"Cozy. But it would be nicer if you were in this bed with me."

"Um," she replied, glad for the room's darkness.

"Anyway, Yance gave everybody lunch, picnic-style, and I managed to nab a plate without anyone noticing."

"Figures."

"I'm a growing boy. Anyway, we loaded up again and drove to the Stuart ranch to look it over. Stephen and John are looking for a good mix of mountains and flats, forest and desert, you know. Stuart had what they wanted but not in the right places for their long shots."

He huffed a short bitter laugh. "The Rolling M would be perfect, only we aren't leasing. We're sell-ing."

Heavy silence hung in the room for a long moment.

"So, Cutes, what did *you* do today?"

"Me?"

"You sound guilty," he commented.

"Well, I'm not," she said guiltily. "I'm not at all. Really. I spent the day with you, Caid Matthews."

There was another silence.

"Is that a fact?" Caid finally asked. "And do you think Yance Chisolm is handsome like the rest of the ladies do?"

Marlie's guilt vanished. "Don't be cute. We went swimming in Balmorhea, and coming back, you showed me the rock walls the soldiers built, remember?"

"No."

"Then we went to eat and I brought a plate back to the hotel for you before I took you back to Waldo's truck, only you weren't here."

"A confusion of 'you's. How do you keep all of 'em straight, Cutes?"

"The same way you do. By pretending not to see the obvious."

"I'm not a doppelgänger," he said without missing a beat. "Thanks for bringing me supper. I ate it while you were in the shower. But all this confusion doesn't explain your coming in so late from the state park. Nobody stargazes that long. Besides, the park closes its trails to visitors at night."

Marlie sighed. "Listen to yourself, Caid. *How* do you know I was at the state park, or at the trailhead? For that matter, how do you know that we were watching the stars?"

"You told me."

"No, I didn't."

Her life was becoming one big echo, Marlie thought. Twice tonight she'd had this argument with Caid, literally listening to and repeating many of the same words, yet neither part of him was willing to listen to himself.

"You kissed me," she said suddenly into the darkness.

"I know that."

"No, I mean you *kissed* me," she replied, hoping that if she made Caid jealous of himself, perhaps... Well, perhaps he could reconcile the two parts of himself.

"And I liked it," she tacked on. "A lot."

In the darkness, the other bed didn't so much as rustle.

Caid cleared his throat. "Did I... Did he, I mean. Did he, uh, give you that more you want?"

It wasn't jealousy Marlie heard in his voice. It was a pain so deep it almost broke her heart.

"No," she whispered. "He didn't give me enough."

"I'm sorry," Caid replied, and because it was his heart speaking, she knew that he meant it.

But this time she didn't tell him that he needn't be sorry, that it wasn't his fault. Because it was.

"I'm really tired," she said into the darkness. "I think I'll go to sleep now."

"Me, too." he answered, as much a liar as she. "Good night, Cutes."

"Good night, Caid."

When Caid awakened the following morning it was without the felicity of watching Marlie sensuously become aware of the world. She was already up, standing at the bureau, quietly gathering the clothing she would wear for the day.

"Mornin'," he said.

"Good morning." She didn't look at him.

"Are you going out without me again?"

"I'm going home."

He wasn't surprised. "Your vacation isn't over."

Marlie shot him a look he had no trouble inter-preting.

"My vacation," she said, "never got started. I came here to get over a broken heart. Ha!"

"I suppose there's one good thing to come out of all this," Caid said thoughtfully after a moment.

Marlie headed for the bathroom, clothing in hand. "What?"

"You found out what's-his-name didn't break your heart after all."

He had no trouble interpreting this look either, or the decisive bang of the bathroom door.

When Marlie emerged, he was dressed himself and had a cup of coffee from the downstairs complimen-tary pot waiting for her. They had the routine down pat by now.

She sipped the coffee he'd brought her while she put on her makeup, and he took his turn in the bath-room. By the time he was through shaving, she was putting on her lipstick.

"Are you going to have breakfast before you head out?" he asked, watching her use a tissue to blot it.

"Yes. Do you only think of your stomach?"

"I only think of you," he answered. "But a fella has to eat."

Marlie closed her eyes. "Don't."

"Now who's hiding? You can go wherever you want, Cutes. San Antonio or Timbuktu. You can live and have children with whoever you want. But someday, somehow, you'll come home to me. In the meantime, I can wait.''

She recapped her lipstick with a little snap. ''You do that. I'm going to breakfast.'' And she left the room without looking back once.

How was it, Caid wondered when she was gone, that they both admitted to loving the other, that they both understood the other so well, yet now on what was probably their last day together, they were fighting?

But he knew.

Going to the window, he pulled the curtain aside and watched Marlie cross the street to The Drugstore. She strode purposefully, head high and with her derriere swaying gracefully with her body's movement, the sway he'd like to watch for the rest of his life.

What life? With Marlie gone to San Antonio, what would he do now?

The way he saw it, he had two choices.

One, he could live out his days as the ''ghost of the Hotel Limpia.'' Ghost hunters from across the nation would flock to the place and attempt to exorcise him.

Two, he could live out his days on the Rolling M, ashamed to hold his head up around his peers.

Marlie entered The Drugstore, and Caid dropped the curtain to turn back into the empty hotel room.

Well, hell.

Chapter Eleven

"Would you mind taking me out to the ranch?"

Marlie, in the act of pulling her suitcase from the bottom of the wardrobe, glanced up sharply.

Caid sat on the side of the bed, lining up sausages across the bottom of the foam container holding his breakfast. Other than that, his meal looked untouched.

"Now?"

He shrugged. "Beats watching you pack."

"I guess so," she replied slowly. It also beat packing in front of the man she wanted nothing more than to cling to for the next century or so.

Which meant, of course, that it was she who had to watch *him* pack. Although, packing was not what she would call it.

The normally fastidious cowboy tossed shirts and jeans, socks and underwear any old way into his duffel bag, then ruthlessly squashed the contents down to zip it.

Marlie's breakfast sat like a lead weight in the bottom of her stomach.

Finally, he picked up his bag and she picked up her purse and keys. Together they headed for the door. Caid opened it for her.

Unable to help herself, Marlie glanced up at him. In this room they'd met, become best friends, become lovers in the deepest meaning of the word.

"You forgot your hat," she said.

Without a word, Caid returned to the dresser to get it, but didn't put it on right away. Instead, he looked at it for a long moment, at the two identical feathers marching side by side in its hatband.

"Do you want your feather back?" he asked finally.

Getting over this man would be difficult enough without that particular reminder, she thought, and shook her head.

Caid placed the hat on his head, picked up his bag again, and they left the room. Marlie locked it behind them.

They hardly spoke as they made the long trip to the Rolling M, following Limpia Creek for a way in the opposite direction than they'd driven yesterday.

As they headed further into the mountains, Marlie spied the domes of McDonald Observatory, one of the sights she hadn't seen. But then, Caid had given her his own version of a star party. The thought of the Big Dipper would still be giving her heart palpitations when she was eighty.

On past the scene of Caid's accident, where she'd spilled onto his broad shoulder all her pent-up hurt over her job and her loss of whatshisname. And where

Caid had wanted to kiss her and didn't, he'd said, but later more than made up for the omission.

Today, neither of them commented.

Finally they turned in the gate to the Rolling M, to bounce and climb their way to its main buildings where Caid had kissed her for the first time, and she'd had an inkling that life as she knew it was about to take a radical turn.

And there was the big house. And there was Caid about to climb into Waldo's old truck. He stood beside its open door, watching her as she pulled up behind it in her SUV.

With the dust from her approach roiling around the two vehicles, she stayed behind the wheel for a moment to give it time to settle.

But as it billowed around them, cocooning them for a brief moment from the world outside, Caid, the one sitting beside her, took off his hat.

"I guess it's his after all," he said quietly, handing it to her. "It's a tough thing, breaking up your land and putting an old friend out to pasture. It's even tougher living with yourself when you do it."

With the dust beginning to settle around them, through the windshield they could see Caid, beating his old straw hat against his thigh.

In the SUV, he sighed quietly. "Sometimes, though, like it or not, a man's got to do what a man's got to do."

His mouth quirked in a small sad smile. "Even John Wayne had his back to the wall on occasion. I love you, Marlie."

Without giving her time to reply, he opened the door and left the vehicle.

Marlie looked at the hat in her hand and at Caid, still standing beside Waldo's pickup staring back at her.

The other Caid bent over a deliriously barking Dynamite as Waldo appeared from around a corner, probably to see what all the ruckus was about.

Slowly, she too left the car.

"Hey, Cutes."

"Hey, yourself." For the life of her, Marlie couldn't think what to say next.

She needn't have worried.

"How did you find me? The ranch gate is unmarked."

The man's middle name was suspicion, Marlie thought with an inward sigh. "I've been here before," she said. "In fact, I've brought you home twice now."

He scratched the back of his neck, tilting his hat forward a little. "We're back to that, are we?"

"We never left it. He—you—never mind. Here's the hat," and she handed it to him with a small disgusted shove.

Caid took it reflexively, but as he'd done back at the hotel room, he stared at the two blue feathers in it for a long silent moment. "Thanks," he said at last.

"It's not me you should thank."

"Do you want your feather back?"

"No."

Echoes again. She turned away, ready to head back to town, then remembered something and turned around again.

"Waldo," she called. "Have you ever heard of the Iq'nata tribe?"

The old man held her gaze for a long moment, his face inscrutable. "Maybe."

"Thought so."

Beside her, Marlie felt Caid come to attention. Think on *that* awhile, Mr. Pure Common Sense, she thought.

"Well, I'm off," she tossed out to no one in particular. "Have a good life." She kept that one generic, too.

Before she'd taken two steps, Caid caught her elbow, halting her in her tracks. "Don't be dramatic, Cutes. Come in and have a cup of coffee or something. Have some breakfast."

"I've eaten," she said.

"Well, I haven't. Not much anyway. Wasn't hungry earlier. Besides, I wanted to get a move on, catch you in town before you went out."

Marlie blinked. "Why?"

He grinned the heart-stopping grin that tripped her heart up every time. "Thought we might ride down to Big Bend Park and dip our toes in the Rio Grande. You wouldn't want to miss that, would you?"

"I'm afraid I'll have to," Marlie replied. More time with this cowboy was not what she needed to get her life back on track.

"As soon as I finish packing, I'm leaving for home today. But thanks for showing me the fort and the other places and taking me swimming. I enjoyed it," she added politely.

"I didn't show you the fort."

"Whatever." She pulled her elbow from Caid's light grasp and headed for her vehicle again.

"But I will," Caid said quickly. "And anything

else you want to see. Don't go yet, Cutes. Your vacation isn't over.''

"Oh, but it is. And it's time for me to go home.''

"Marlie, please.'' Caid's desperation caught him completely by surprise, but he didn't have time to think about it.

He threw the straw hat into the back of the pickup so he could yank on the one she'd brought him, leaving his hands free to bracket her shoulders. If this woman walked out of his life, it would be a bigger disaster than losing part of his ranch.

"At least have a cup of coffee,'' he said persuasively.

But Marlie must have heard the desperation, too, because she looked up at him, her gray eyes wide and startled.

And then he was lost, caught by the clear purity of her gaze just as he always was.

Just as he wanted to be for the rest of his life.

"Don't go,'' he said. "Stay with me. We're good together, Marlie. You know we are.''

"Marriage, Caid?'' Marlie, direct and to the point, as usual, he thought.

There were parts of her personality that might be hard to live with.

He swallowed. "Well…''

Tell her you love her, you idiot.

Shut up.

"I really, really like you, Marlie. We could make a life with that, couldn't we?''

"No,'' she said. "We couldn't.''

"But we have so much going for us. We like the same jokes. We know how to talk, how to laugh together. We have fun together. Better yet, we enjoy each other's company. That doesn't happen often, now does it?''

"No, it doesn't," she conceded slowly. "But I want more, Caid. I told you that."

"We'll light a bonfire in bed," he said quickly. "We've already proven we have only to touch each other for sparks to fly."

"That's not what I meant. At least, that's not what I meant this time."

She, too, was beginning to sound a little desperate, Caid thought gleefully. He almost had her.

Not marriage, but a...a *relationship*. Wasn't that the current buzz word? A relationship until they got tired of each other.

Not that he saw getting tired of this woman happening in the next couple hundred years.

You're about the stupidest hayseed I ever saw.

What do you know?

"I want your heart, Caid."

Marlie's calm voice silenced him completely. His hands dropped from her shoulders. "You want the one thing I don't have, Cutes," he said at last.

"Yes, you do."

She reached up to touch his cheek, but he took her hand in his and kissed her fingertips before giving it back to her, defeated.

"Go home, Marlie Simms," he said quietly. "You were right. The vacation's over. There's a good man waiting for you somewhere, one far better than what-shisname who couldn't find his back pockets if he sat on a nail. Certainly there's one better for you than me. You deserve a lifetime filled with love."

And he gently kissed her cheek while everything in him wanted to kiss her mouth and haul her off to have breakfast in bed.

Well hell. She has your heart, you nincompoop, and she knows it. But you're the one who has to tell her this time.

Marlie, however, changed the subject on him.

"You've been out of the hospital awhile, Caid. Why haven't you been to the bank?"

"What?"

"You heard me. You haven't been to the real estate office, either. Apparently, you've had plenty of time to show me around, but no time to take care of business. I'm wondering why."

He shrugged. "Just haven't gotten around to it, is all." His eyes narrowed. Why did she want to know?

"Why?" he asked.

Watch it, buster. You know damn good and well Marlie isn't Janice. She doesn't want the land.

Marlie stared right back at him with that laser gaze of hers. "You tell me," she said.

"I asked you first."

When she rolled her eyes, he suddenly understood why Marlie was such a bad liar. The truth had a way of coming out of her mouth like a smart bomb—one of those that never misses its target.

"Because your heart's not in it," she said. "When you had your accident, it stepped out to give you free rein for making those tough decisions. Don't you see? Your heart isn't wimpy, Caid, or cowardly."

He snorted.

"In fact, it's really very noble," Marlie continued, unfazed. "The only way you could do what you had to do was not listen to it anymore, so it took a hike. The thing is, your heart is also your guiding force and without it, you're never going to get much done.''

Caid looked at the sky, hoping for divine intervention.

''There's no help there,'' Marlie said smartly. ''Your heart is behind you giving Dynamite the ear rub of his life.''

He didn't bother to check. ''Marlie…''

''Have you told Waldo?''

Now this was going too far.

''Told me what?'' Waldo asked.

''Nothing,'' Caid said. ''Marlie…''

''Better yet, have you *asked* Waldo?''

Now, Cutes, I thought you told me you were through meddling in other people's business.

''You told me I can meddle in yours,'' Marlie replied. ''Besides, I love you.''

Caid grabbed her shoulders, a big goofy grin on his face. ''Marlie…''

''Asked me what?'' Waldo asked.

''If you'd like to retire,'' Marlie told him, but stared into Caid's frozen features. Caid dropped her shoulders like a hot poker.

Frozen features, hot poker. Get it? Marlie wanted to weep.

''Well, I might,'' the old man drawled.

That got their attention. Everyone but Marlie stared at him.

Waldo scratched under his chin. ''Been thinkin' about it for some time now,'' he said slowly. ''These bones are gettin' kinda stiff. Thing is, I don't want to go to Florida. The Rollin' M's my *home.*''

Marlie could tell Waldo was trying his best to sound pathetic…and was doing a darn good job of it.

"Well hell, Waldo, you don't have to leave the ranch if you don't want to. You can retire and stay right here. The Rolling M will always have a place for you."

Some of that was Caid's heart talking, Marlie was glad to note. The other part of him probably wanted to wring her neck.

While his attention was on Waldo, Marlie sidled into the SUV and slammed the door, locking it for good measure.

The motor was running by the time he realized what she'd done. She lowered the window to half-mast.

"Movies," she called out of it as she slowly backed up. "Hollywood money."

She swung the SUV around and pointed it down the road. "Mountains and flats, desert and forest," she yelled through the swirling dust.

"Lease," she hollered out the window at the top of her lungs, and left Caid, his heart, Waldo and Dynamite staring after her in the ranch yard.

"Well, hell," Caid said, once the dust had settled.

You let her get away, you fool. Here I thought you had some sense and you let the only woman I'll ever love drive off without so much as a goodbye.

"Me? I didn't hear you making your presence known. The woman needed to hear sweet talk."

The woman needed to hear commitment, you jackass. Give me my hat. Since you don't have the sense God gave a large-size tomato, I'm going after her.

Caid reached up, pulled his hat more firmly on his head, and set his jaw. "No, you don't. *I'm* going."

"If you'd stop arguin' with yourself," Waldo said mildly, "you might notice you've got a problem."

Caid looked in the direction of Waldo's terse nod toward the pickup.

Well, hell.

He had a flat.

Marlie folded a blouse, blew her nose and packed the garment neatly into her suitcase. She tucked a pair of rolled socks into each of her hiking boots, placed the rest around the edges, then swiped at her eyes with a raised shoulder.

This time there was no Caid, either of him, to take her in his arms and make her feel better.

With nothing left to pack, she stared at her filled suitcase bleakly for a moment, then made a final round of the room looking for anything she might have missed.

Bureau drawers, empty. Wardrobe, nothing. Bathroom, not so much as a used razor blade. Under the bed, a gum wrapper. Her own.

Caid hadn't left a thing, darn it. She blinked back a fresh spate of tears.

The only remains of him that she'd found was his congealed uneaten breakfast. That didn't seem quite the thing to tuck away in a box full of memories, however.

Slowly she closed the suitcase and fastened it. She should have kept her feather.

Grammie had said the man she'd find in West Texas was not necessarily her destiny, that it was her choice to take him or leave him. Well, she was leaving him.

Admittedly, she'd been half hoping one or the other of him would rush into town and stop her.

Better yet, both of them. One Caid to rush up the stairs, throw his hat on the bed and throw Marlie on the other. One Caid to rush up the stairs, throw his hat on the bed and throw his heart at Marlie's feet.

The inescapable fact was, though, that if both Caids rushed up the stairs, they would probably do nothing but argue with each other. Marlie was tired of being a referee.

Leave it to her, she thought, to love a man who wouldn't accept his own heart.

How, then, could he truly accept hers?

Picking up her suitcase, she left the room and didn't look back.

Ann was at the desk when she went to check out.

"Does Caid know you're leaving?" the desk clerk asked as she processed Marlie's credit card.

Marlie tried for a cheerful smile. "Oh, yes," she replied brightly, tacking on for good measure, "Fort Davis is a wonderful place." That much, at least, was true. "I've, uh, really had a-a w-wonderful time."

In spite of herself, she hiccupped.

"That good, huh?" Ann handed her the receipt to sign. "We've enjoyed having you. Do you think you'll ever get back this way?"

Not in this lifetime, Marlie thought. She smiled politely around her damp tissue. "Maybe."

"And maybe definitely," Ann said, looking past

her to the hotel's main entrance. "Here comes the cavalry."

Marlie turned to see what Ann was talking about, and would have lost her heart if she hadn't left it in pieces in the room upstairs.

"Oh no, it isn't," she told Ann, her tears drying like magic under the onslaught of renewed determination. "I'm not taking home any souvenirs."

Picking up her bag, she marched past Caid and out the door he'd left open behind him.

On the hotel's wide front porch, Caid plucked the suitcase from her hand. "Marlie..."

"Is this here cowboy giving you trouble, little lady?"

A leather-clad biker slowly rose from one of the hotel's porch rockers. Judging by the lurid tattoo of a voluptuous naked woman running up one beefy forearm and the fire-breathing dragon flowing around the other, he wasn't a preacher.

"Yes," Marlie said.

"I am not," Caid said indignantly.

The biker took a threatening step forward.

Caid dropped her suitcase so he could spread his arms appealingly. "I drove fifty miles into town just to tell the lady that I love her and she won't stop long enough to listen," he told the biker. "Can you beat that? And I had to change a tire to do it."

"No reasoning with some women," the biker said, sitting down again. "If I was you, I'd find another one."

Marlie rolled her eyes. Men! Didn't they all stick together.

Grabbing her bag, she headed down the porch steps....

"I thought of that, but my heart's stuck on this one."

That stopped her.

"I'm hoping she'll see that I've, uh, got my act together," Caid added.

She turned...

"Hot sweaty sex and X-rated rolls in the hay."

"Hoo-boy," the biker said.

"Kids. Love. Lots of love." He paused. "I love you, Marlie Simms."

She dropped her suitcase. "Caid?"

In three long strides, he was off the porch and had her in his arms. "That's me," he said.

And it was. Looking up at him, Marlie saw his heart in his eyes. "Oh, Caid," she managed before his mouth found hers.

Love, seering passion and peace. It was all there, just as she'd dreamed.

When they finally came up for air, he plopped his hat on her head. "Marry me," he commanded.

"Wellll..."

"I do declare, little lady! You can say 'well' at a time like *this?*" the biker growled. "What are you? Made outta rock?"

"I want a prenuptial agreement."

"What!" The biker and Caid looked at each other in consternation.

"A prenuptial agreement," she repeated patiently.

"Marlie, honey, a prenuptial agreement is nothing but trouble. The Chisolms had one and it almost wrecked their marriage. I trust you. I really do."

"That's your heart talking," Marlie replied with a small smile. "The rest of you isn't all that sure. Your first wife hurt you badly and the wound's still fresh."

She cupped his face between her two hands. "It's just a piece of paper, Caid, to act as a bandage, that's all. It'll say I don't want your ranch ever, unless you're on it. We'll toss the thing when we don't need it anymore."

"If that's what you want, Cutes. But we've got something a whole lot better, you know."

Reaching up, he removed the hat from her head so that she could see the two blue feathers in the hat-band.

"We've got the Great Ones' seal of approval," he said seriously, then grinned. "But if you really want a prenup, we'll do that, too."

And he replaced the hat on her head.

Marlie pushed it up off her nose. A woman knows she's loved, she thought, when a cowboy gives her his hat.

"Now that we've settled that, let's find some breakfast. Heck, it's almost time for lunch. I'm so hungry I could eat a leather jacket."

"Watch it there, bud," the biker called.

Marlie, tucked under Caid's arm, waved at him.

He waggled a couple of sausage fingers back.

The corner of her mouth tilted; Caid's eyebrow quirked.

"Breakfast," Caid said. "Then we need to find John and Stephen. You know, the film people? That acreage I was thinking about selling would be perfect for what they have in mind, and if I lease it to 'em, I won't have to sell."

"Really?"

He grinned. "Really. You're a smart cookie, Cutes. And I'm always hungry."

"Hey," the biker called out. "Good one."

* * * * *

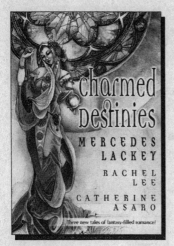

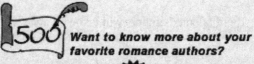

✂

Your opinion is important to us! Please take a few moments to share your thoughts with us about your experiences with Harlequin and Silhouette books. Your comments will be very useful in ensuring that we deliver books you love to read.
Please take a few minutes to complete the questionnaire, then send it to us at the address below.

Send your completed questionnaires to:
Harlequin/Silhouette Reader Survey, P.O. Box 9046, Buffalo, NY 14269-9046

---

1. As you may know, there are many different lines under the Harlequin and Silhouette brands. Each of the lines is listed below. Please check the box that most represents your reading habit for each line.

Line	Currently read this line	Do not read this line	Not sure if I read this line
Harlequin American Romance	❏	❏	❏
Harlequin Duets	❏	❏	❏
Harlequin Romance	❏	❏	❏
Harlequin Historicals	❏	❏	❏
Harlequin Superromance	❏	❏	❏
Harlequin Intrigue	❏	❏	❏
Harlequin Presents	❏	❏	❏
Harlequin Temptation	❏	❏	❏
Harlequin Blaze	❏	❏	❏
Silhouette Special Edition	❏	❏	❏
Silhouette Romance	❏	❏	❏
Silhouette Intimate Moments	❏	❏	❏
Silhouette Desire	❏	❏	❏

2. Which of the following best describes why you bought *this book?* One answer only, please.

the picture on the cover	❏	the title	❏
the author	❏	the line is one I read often	❏
part of a miniseries	❏	saw an ad in another book	❏
saw an ad in a magazine/newsletter	❏	a friend told me about it	❏
I borrowed/was given this book	❏	other: _____	❏

3. Where did you buy *this book?* One answer only, please.

at Barnes & Noble	❏	at a grocery store	❏
at Waldenbooks	❏	at a drugstore	❏
at Borders	❏	on eHarlequin.com Web site	❏
at another bookstore	❏	from another Web site	❏
at Wal-Mart	❏	Harlequin/Silhouette Reader	❏
at Target	❏	Service/through the mail	
at Kmart	❏	used books from anywhere	❏
at another department store or mass merchandiser	❏	I borrowed/was given this book	❏

4. On average, how many Harlequin and Silhouette books do you buy at one time?

I buy _____ books at one time ❏
I rarely buy a book ❏

MRQ403SR-1A

5. How many times per month do you shop for any *Harlequin and/or Silhouette* books?
   One answer only, please.

1 or more times a week	❑	a few times per year	❑
1 to 3 times per month	❑	less often than once a year	❑
1 to 2 times every 3 months	❑	never	❑

6. When you think of your ideal heroine, which *one* statement describes her the best?
   One answer only, please.

She's a woman who is strong-willed	❑	She's a desirable woman	❑
She's a woman who is needed by others	❑	She's a powerful woman	❑
She's a woman who is taken care of	❑	She's a passionate woman	❑
She's an adventurous woman	❑	She's a sensitive woman	❑

7. The following statements describe types or genres of books that you may be
   interested in reading. Pick *up to 2 types* of books that you are most interested in.

I like to read about truly romantic relationships	❑
I like to read stories that are sexy romances	❑
I like to read romantic comedies	❑
I like to read a romantic mystery/suspense	❑
I like to read about romantic adventures	❑
I like to read romance stories that involve family	❑
I like to read about a romance in times or places that I have never seen	❑
Other: _____	❑

*The following questions help us to group your answers with those readers who are
similar to you. Your answers will remain confidential.*

8. Please record your year of birth below.

   19 _____

9. What is your marital status?

   single ❑   married ❑   common-law ❑   widowed ❑
   divorced/separated ❑

10. Do you have children 18 years of age or younger currently living at home?

    yes ❑   no ❑

11. Which of the following best describes your employment status?

    employed full-time or part-time ❑   homemaker ❑   student ❑
    retired ❑   unemployed ❑

12. Do you have access to the Internet from either home or work?

    yes ❑   no ❑

13. Have you ever visited eHarlequin.com?

    yes ❑   no ❑

14. What state do you live in?

    _____

15. Are you a member of Harlequin/Silhouette Reader Service?

    yes ❑   Account # _____   no ❑   MRQ403SR-1B

COMING NEXT MONTH

#1694 FILL-IN FIANCÉE—DeAnna Talcott
Marrying the Boss's Daughter

Recruiting well-mannered beauty Sunny Robbins to pose as his bride-to-be was the perfect solution to Lord Breton Hamilton's biggest problem—his matchmaking parents! Sunny wasn't the titled English aristocrat they expected, but she was a more enticing alternative than *their* choices. And the way she sent his pulse racing… Was Brett's fill-in fiancée destined to become his lawfully—*lovingly*—wedded wife?

#1695 THE PRINCESS & THE MASKED MAN—
Valerie Parv
The Carramer Trust

Beautiful royals didn't propose marriages of convenience! Yet that's exactly what Princess Giselle de Marigny did when she discovered Bryce Laws's true identity. Since the widowed single father wanted a mother for his young daughter, he agreed to the plan. But Giselle's kisses stirred deeper feelings, and Bryce realized she might become keeper of his heart!

#1696 TO WED A SHEIK—Teresa Southwick
Desert Brides

Crown Prince Kamal Hassan promised never to succumb to the weakness of love, but Ali Matlock, his sexy new employee, was tempting him beyond all limits. The headstrong American had made it clear an office fling was out of the question. But for Kamal, so was giving up Ali. Would he trade his playboy lifestyle for a lifetime of happiness?

#1697 WEST TEXAS BRIDE—Madeline Baker
City girl Carly Kirkwood had about as much business on a Texas ranch as she did falling for rancher Zane Roan Eagle— none! Still, she couldn't deny her attraction to the handsome cowboy or the sparks that flew between them. Would she be able to leave the big city behind for Zane? And could she forgive him when the secrets of his past were revealed?